A Rose by Any Other Name

A Beyond Fairytales story

By
Landra Graf

~A Note from the Author~

Dear Readers,

Zombies are my greatest fear. Psychos and serial killers, I can handle. Insects or wild animals, I'll find a way. Zombies... nope, I'm out of here. So when my close friend encouraged me to write a fairy-tale re-telling of Sleeping Beauty plus zombies, I knew this would be my greatest challenge yet. Throw a romance into the mix and I thought... impossible. In the end I found a way to make the whole story come together, and give Sleeping Beauty a different twist. At least, Beauty doesn't get the prince this time.

I hope you enjoyed the story, and applaud you for being brave enough to read the book that put me on edge as I wrote in the quiet, night hours.

As always, I love to hear what my readers think. So, drop me a line at landra.graf7@gmail.com

Sincerely,
Landra

Dedication

To my critique partner, Lori, for pushing me to write outside of my comfort zone and always being there for me. Friend, I would've never made it this far with you. Thanks for the multiple years and I pray for a gazillion more.

Prologue

"Why, how now, good mother," said the
princess. "What are you doing there?"

Emmaline Fay sat down on a plywood bench in
front of the *Storytelling Spectacular* stage and
sighed. Draped and twirled around light posts,
dozens of light strings lit up the high school parking
lot. Vendor carts were positioned throughout,
surrounded by a Ferris wheel, pendulum ride, and
flying swings. Carousel music and squeals of delight
rang out to her left as people young and old clung to
painted horses or sat on dragon seats. Carnies yelled
out invitations at the students milling around, and
the sweet smell of funnel cakes filled the air.

She'd arrived early, and her best bet at being
located by her friends involved staying in the center
of the school fair. The May night ran a bit chilly, so
she pulled on the edges of her jean jacket, the effort
out of habit rather than actually generating warmth.
Right then, the stage curtains parted, the bucket
lights rimming the edge of the platform casting an
eerie glow over the warped wood. An old, short,
gnome-like man hobbled to a three-legged stool in

1

the center of the elevated setting. He wore shabby clothes, and a long, silver beard flowed past his waist.

After a slow totter, he finally sat, stroking his beard and placing the barrel of a pipe between his lips. "Welcome, young and old. Sit and let me tell you a tale. For a small price, of course."

Those words prompted a few of the folks at the front to drop coins into a glass jar poised on the edge of the stage. Emmaline didn't hear them hit due to the noise from the fairway behind her, but the money put a smile on the man's face. "Thank ye kindly. My name be Nicodemus, and I have a tale of woe to share. Once upon a time—"

"Emma, I've been looking for you everywhere." The words, uttered by her best friend in the whole world, were paired with two hands gripping the back of her jacket and tugging hard. She went with the motion, rotating her body to the left and bringing her legs over the bench to stand.

"He just got started. We should stay for the story."

Rose, all five foot three, long blonde locks, and pouty lips, grinned the big grin she used to try to convince and bargain with others. It worked nearly every time. "But Jason found a fortune teller, and he's holding our spot in line. We have to go. Maybe she'll tell us how many kids we'll have."

Before she could object, her friend took off, skipping through the throng of people, and Em followed like she always did. They both came to a stop in front of a six-foot-tall patched tent monstrosity with Tiki torches and a braided, multi-colored rug spread out in front of the entrance like a welcome mat.

"Why are we doing this?" She dug her heels into the ground, a last ditch attempt to avoid the tent.

Rose giggled, "For fun, silly."

The whole event screamed fake and a waste of cash. Her mind desperately searched for an excuse to not participate when the smell of linen laundry soap, summer, and berries filled her nostrils—a unique scent known to haunt her dreams and waking hours, thanks to a flannel shirt Jason had left at her house a few weeks ago.

"Ladies, ready to discover our future? Or at least how many touchdowns I'll score playing for Wisconsin?" Jason Prince, the most handsome guy in Charming, Iowa, stepped in front of them, smiling wide. He'd also become one of the most arrogant, but even a flaw like that didn't make him unlovable.

3

Treating her best friend and, by extension, her, like a queen also earned him brownie points.

"Wow, you sure know how to keep that ego in check," said Rose. No response came from the jock beyond the waggling eyebrows and a female squeal as he pulled his girlfriend into a bear hug.

Emma did her best during displays of affection to remain neutral, but it still hurt in ways she'd never tell anyone. "All right, I'm in, but only if you two will quit the touchy-feely stuff until after the reading and no offers for godmothering are on the table."

Rose broke away from her man and wrapped her arms around her. "Thank you, Em. We can keep it clean until after, but no promises on the godmother thing."

"Next up," a carnie called from the tent entrance.

As a group, they stepped forward past the beaded curtain and into a dimly lit area, their shadows casting strange shapes against the walls. The whole ambience called for slow and cautious movement. Then the voice.... "Come in, children." The grandmother's croak made Emma shiver. Her friends, on the other hand, continued forward, chuckling. They weren't creeped out; if anything, the spooky atmosphere enhanced their excitement, but not her. No, she didn't find humor in "scary." "Guys, I'm going to—"

"You can't back out now, scaredy cat," Jason said, securing a hand around her wrist. "I already paid. Don't worry. I can protect you both."

She shook her head but didn't resist. When it came to arguments, she didn't put up much of a fight. Instead, she settled for insults. "Moron."

Rickety chairs were positioned around a table covered in some silky red fabric. Rose sat down first. They flanked her, sitting on either side. Only then did Emmaline glance at the supposed fortune teller, who looked like Mrs. Wiggs, the high school janitor.

The woman was ready for a performance. A couple of long, stringy strands of gray hair were visible from beneath some sort of dark colored cloak, dozens of bangles dangled from her wrinkly arms, and she wore enough makeup to put a beauty shop out of business.

Ever the practical one, Emma decided to not waste any time. "My friend would like a reading, please."

Stormy gray eyes met hers, and the old woman replied, "Certainly. Which one of you?"

"Me. I want the reading." Rose bowed her head,

hands on her purse. A shimmer of gold reflected in the light as she undid the clasp. "Do you need something personal?"

"No, my dear. Just a palm, preferably the one you write with." Abandoning the purse at her side, the reigning prom queen extended her right hand.

Emmaline attempted to contain a laugh. Rose and Jason seemed completely enraptured by the sight of this woman's liver-spotted and wrinkled fingers wrapped around her creamy white ones. As soon as the two hands met at the middle of the table, the old woman's head pitched forward. The effect proved creepy as hell. Momentarily, Emma thought the woman was experiencing a seizure as her entire body shivered and shook.

They all let out a collective gasp, but she edged her chair back, one leg snagging in the carpet laid over the grass. "Guys, let's get out of—"

"Ten years," the woman's voice rasped. Her head rose from the table, the hood of her cloak falling backward, eyes unfocused. "Ten years. Upon such time passing, you will find a prick to bring harm to the world."

Immaturity reigned as the jock snorted. "I've never been known to do that."

"Hush, you idiot. She's not talking about that." Emma reached behind her friend to swat him on the arm. "What do you mean prick?"

"A needle...and then a great sickness will be upon us. Beware! This path cannot be altered."

The woman's head pitched forward again, and Rose snatched her hand back. Jason cradled her against him, comforting her, and, just like that, the fun and games were over.

Emma dealt with the look of fear on her friend's face in the best possible way—with humor. "Gotcha."

"Baby, you okay?"

Instead of answering her boyfriend, Rose forced a chuckle. "Senior year practical joke.... Huh, Em?"

"Tricked you good, didn't I?" Of course, she'd never do anything like that, but she'd protected her friend many times before, and another small lie made no difference.

"Yep, you got me. Let's go ride the Ferris wheel." Thank goodness she was a ray of sunshine and hope and could never stay down for long.

"All for it, babe." Jason helped his girl out of her seat and through the hanging beads. He gave Emma a look implying they'd be talking later.

One last glance at Mrs. Wiggs. A chill stole over

her as the woman pointed a bony finger at her friend's retreating backside and hissed, "Sickness."

She turned away with half a mind to tell her father about how his janitor had acted toward them. Fortunes weren't supposed to give people nightmares. They were supposed to display happy expectations, or at least fake them.

Chapter One

"How prettily that little thing turns round!" said the princess, and took the spindle and began to spin.

Ten years later.

"When will you get here?"

The sound of excitement in Rose's voice at the prospect of her coming home raised Emma's spirits. She hadn't gone back in three years, not since the factory shut down. "It'll take about six hours, so maybe around six."

"Ooh, I can't wait. There's a pre-reunion party at Sound Awake tonight."

"That bar is still open?"

"Yes, can you believe it? Oh my gosh. You're really coming," Rose squealed.

Emma pulled the phone away from her ear about two inches, but echoed with a similar sentiment. "I'm coming for sure. Meet up at your place by six thirty?"

"Sure thing. This is going to be a weekend to remember, especially if Jason shows up. I'll just finish my rounds and— *Ow.*"

1

A twinge of dread swept through Emma like a memory clamoring to break the surface. Concerned, she called out, "Rose? What happened?"

"I'm fine." A sucking sound flitted through the phone. "Just jabbed myself with one of Mr. Delphi's needles. Went straight through my glove. It'll be fine with a Band-Aid. I've done worse."

Only a needle. The town beauty queen was known for accidents. She never came away with any damages other than the occasional bandage or wrap, but whether it was falling into holes or colliding with objects directly in her path, she always needed a close eye and a hero.

"I'm going to get off the phone with you, so you can finish working without distractions."

"All right, but one more question?"

"Shoot."

A deep exhale came over the line, "Do you think Jason will be there?"

The breakup hadn't been bitter, but she knew eight years had failed to change her friend's feelings about the one who got away. The mention of his name even sent a little chill of excitement coursing through her own veins. She shook off the idea of her old high school crush. Jason and Rose belonged together. "If he is, I hope he's prepared for you to knock him off his feet."

"Aww, you're the best. Well, I'll get off the phone now, but you'd better call as soon as you hit city limits."

"Will do."

The hours rolled by, and the familiar giddiness at the idea of returning home became stronger with each passing mile marker. Some people said home was where your clothes were, but she knew home to be the place of all her memories. Driving the back roads far away from the cities and into the no man's land of Iowa, she recalled the days when her ultimate goal involved getting as far away from small town life as possible. She wasn't the prom queen or the smartest girl in school, but the daughter of the high school principal and best friend to the sweetest person who ever lived. Escaping the comforts of country life, she went running to the city two months into her last summer as a kid. Until this moment, she hadn't looked back.

As she finally passed the *Welcome to Charming* sign, she rolled down the window, taking in the sweet scent of sunflowers growing in the big beds around the town marker.

Set on either side of the road, a row of once cherry-red, white roofed cottages—now weathered with age, their paint faded and peeling—always reminded her of big barns and served as tribute to farm country. The four houses were once rented out to tourists with the exception of the first one, which belonged to the town gossip and gatekeeper. Emma stepped on the brakes, slowing down to talk with said gossip.

"Hi, Emmaline." Mrs. Hopkins offered the greeting with a wave from her chair on the front porch. Not a single person could sneak into town without the obligatory wave since, like a castle village from olden times, there was only one way in and one way out of Charming.

"Hi. How'd you know it was me?"

"That hair is your mother's, black as a raven. Since I saw her an hour ago, and we talked about your visit, it makes sense."

"You're right. It's good to see you," she replied, summoning up her skills of polite conversation. Mrs. Hopkins, her mother's closet companion and confidant, would alert every one of her arrival, a reminder of why she enjoyed city life where people came and went as they pleased without causing a stir

4

or inciting concern.

"You, too, dear. Be slow. Remember the speed limit."

She sighed at the reminder, spouted out to each visitor and resident. In the old days, Mrs. Hopkins also used to mention, "Watch out for children."

As she passed each street, there were more signs that idyllic Charming had fallen in stature and no longer resembled the town she'd once roamed. Faded signs, cracked paint, and for sale signs littered the main strip. The hardware store and pharmacy were still operating, though the post office had a sign announcing new part-time hours, and the local diner only stayed open until three in the afternoon now. When she was a teenager, the diner had served ice cream and fried goodness deep into the night, especially on Fridays after football and basketball games. She'd worked at the flower shop next door, conducting deliveries, but it had shut down when the owner moved out of state to be closer to her daughter.

Turning off the main road, she pulled out her phone to dial Rose.

"Hello—"

"Hey, just got into—" She cut off at the sound of

Rose's voice rambling on.

"You've reached Rose Briar, hospice nurse for Mason's Family Practice. If this is an emergency, dial 911 or call Dr. Mason. Otherwise, leave a message at the tone."

With a sigh, Emma continued, "Just got into town. Things look a heck of a lot different. You and Daddy never told me that we're down to one gas station. Anyways, still planning to swing by in, oh... about an hour. You'd better be ready." With a snap of the phone and twist of the key, she exited her vehicle, purse in hand. She stopped and stared for a minute at the two-story farmhouse in front of her, the tire swing still hanging from the big oak in the front yard. They'd twirled each other on that swing clear through high school. Things had been simpler then.

The memories buoyed her, and she grabbed her bag from the backseat of her Ford Taurus on a wave of child-like energy. A few quick steps from the yard to the front porch and she spotted the heart-shaped doorbell her mom claimed was proof the house was filled with love. She rang the bell.

Someone's shoes shuffled across the floor on the other side of the door, followed by her mother's distinctive, high-pitched squeal. "Ooh, Herb, hurry.

6

She's here."

The door flung open, and she threw herself into Mom's arms. Her father lumbered down the hall, his six-foot-frame equipped with the standard professor cardigan, button-down shirt, and reading glasses perched on his Roman nose. "Here you are. Home at last."

"Well, of course she is. You say that like she's a ghost or something," Edie Fay scolded as she pulled out of Emma's embrace. "Turn around, dear. Look at you in that fancy suit. Chicago's treating you well."

She smiled. "Yes, so good I can buy slacks and a jacket like any self-respecting chemical engineer. It's not that impressive."

"I'm sorry. I know I exaggerate things, but your father and I are proud of you. Now, when will we meet the boyfriend?"

"There isn't one." Mom always brought up the topics she didn't want to discuss.

Dad wrapped her in a hug; he usually followed with questions she didn't want to answer. "Does it matter? She's home for once, and I'm glad we don't have to entertain someone else." She caught her dad's wink as he released her from the hug. "What have you been up to, though, if there isn't a man?"

And here we go. They'd been bugging her for months to come home. For holidays, for a quick stay, whatever they thought of, the idea got hurled her way. The fact that her parents failed to see how happy the city and her engineering job made her hurt. What hurt more was their lack of interest in visiting her on her home turf, opting to push for home field advantage every time. "Working. Testing a new product with the qualities of ammonia. Complicated and too boring to talk about all night."

She repositioned her purse straps and took stock of the new prints her mother had put on the walls along with the new shade of daisy yellow brightening the hallway. There were other reasons she couldn't discuss her job in detail, including the massive non-disclosure agreement she'd signed. The potential to re-open old wounds and ignite her typical parental issues was another.

Mom patted her on the shoulder. "I'm sure your father will want to hear all about it over breakfast. For now, we'll let you get ready."

"Ready? I'm not in a hurry. It's okay."

Both parents let out a laugh that echoed through the house. Her dad raised his eyebrow. "Three years doesn't change anything. We know when you're ready to get a move on. When are you meeting Rose?"

"I'm supposed to pick her up from her place at six thirty."

"Oh, Then we'd better let you get ready. It's already six. You don't want to be late," her mom said, putting a hand on Emma's back.

The enthusiasm on her face was a bit too "I've got something planned."

"What did you do?"

"Nothing, dear," she replied, walking past, headed for the kitchen at the end of the hall.

"Don't be too upset. You know she just wants the best for you."

"If the best is me marrying some grownup football jock who never looked at me in high school and owns a farm, I'd rather pass. There's no work for a chemical engineer here. If Charming Chemicals hadn't closed down, I would have moved back after UI." She looked up at her father, hoping her expression said "make Mom back off."

"I know, I know. It's not easy since the plant closed, and we're just an old folks' town now. We need a way to draw the young people back." Dad gave her a couple of soft pats on her shoulder. "I'm just glad you're home, finally. Get your stuff up to your room and then make a getaway while I keep your mom busy. You can spend time with us tomorrow."

"I plan on it."

She smiled and gave her dad another hug. It didn't seem to matter how often they annoyed her or how much they wanted her living in Charming, she enjoyed their pestering on some level. Those moments made everything right in the world and the years they'd been apart fade into the background like she'd never left.

The carpet soft on her heels, she recalled the dozens of times she and Rose had raced the stairs with Jason chasing behind them. Yes, he'd always been coming after her friend, not her, but the thrill of the chase had still made her heart pound. Reaching her bedroom, she took a deep breath to stave off the butterflies swamping her stomach. Would the room be different or just like she remembered it?

Opening the door, she caught the smells, the sights—all the same from her light-blue walls with clamshell trim to the four-poster canopy bed Mr. Wilkes, their next-door neighbor, had built her as a birthday present when she turned twelve. Even the smell of fall fields mixed with apples wafting through the room confirmed this place as her home, the same home she'd been so desperate to escape.

Throwing her suitcase on the bed, she shut the door and let the memories swallow her. The pastel yellow dresser next to the closet held emotional markers, mementos from childhood adventures. She picked up the picture of her, Rose, and Jason at the senior carnival, one of the last times they'd spent all night together, playing games, laughing, and being carefree. He'd been gorgeous back then, and she hoped he'd lost some of those boyish good looks. No doubt her bestie would love him no matter what, but she couldn't stand up against his deep-blue eyes. When he trained them on her, her good sense was swallowed up like the waves of the ocean gobbling up off-balance surfers. Her hands traced over his face and then moved on to the jewelry box where she found her "best friends forever" rose-shaped necklace. Its partner rested on Rose's neck. Her fingers grasped at more pieces of history— the New Kids on the Block ticket stubs, their first concert, and at least a half- dozen other trinkets from their years together. They'd spent every weekend in each other's pockets and tormenting relatives since they'd been five-years-old. Nothing could keep them apart, not even a boy. But her friend hadn't known about her infatuation, and, as far as Emma was concerned, she never would.

She slid into jeans and a wrap-around purple top. Her slinky black dress had been the original outfit of the evening, but a sudden inspiration to save that for the reunion had come over her. Brown boots replaced the two-inch heels she'd shown up in. Being home called for shoes fit for traipsing in fields.

As she said good night to her folks and slid behind the wheel, her purse started vibrating, the muffled sound of a trumpet belting out "La Vie En Rose" playing in the background.

"Hey, gal. I'm just getting ready to leave Mom and Dad's driveway to get you."

Rose coughed. "That's funny. My perfect timing. I wanted to tell you to go on without me. It took me a little longer to wrap things up. I just got home."

There was a note of happiness in her friend's tone, but her words seemed labored.

"All right, but are you okay?"

"Perfectly fine. How about you find us a table, and I'll be there in an hour, tops. Oh, snickerdoodles."

Emma frowned at the alternative way of cursing. The girl truly existed on another plane. Her heart went into pounding mode when she heard a clatter followed by the steady hum of static.

"Sorry, dropped the phone. I'm back."

"What the hell happened?"

"Chipped a nail. This reunion and possibly seeing Jason again. I'm fumbling and stumbling all over the place." Rose let out a laugh. "Clumsy as ever, I guess."

"You're not clumsy. You're a student of the graceful art of drop-itsu." She chuckled. "Now, get ready. See you soon."

***

Emma pulled into a spot a block away from Sound Awake, since the tavern parking lot was crowded with cars and people. In her high school days, members of the Masonic Lodge and American Legion had used the bar for meetings and to escape their families. Now it'd become the local hot spot, taking the place of the diner.

She'd picked out a few folks from forensics class, but hesitated when it came to getting out of the car. Nerves from limited social interaction held her back. Hanging out with people wasn't her strong suit, which lent credence to why the last ten years had included two dates and one boyfriend who'd loved her, but not her career or the amount of time her job took up. Instead of hanging with friends or looking for a husband, she'd made big bucks researching ways to transform dangerous waste into benign substances. While her bank account had grown, her social life had taken a dive and—

That's when she saw him, and, damn—he looked better than he had in high school. Back then, he'd been equal proportions of muscle on top and bottom, but since then his shoulders and upper body had filled out.

He looked like a bronzed god. Even though it was fall, he still sported a tan, his blonde hair a shade lighter than she remembered, most likely from time spent outside. Seeing him sparked errant thoughts of finding out what he was doing now. His eyes connected with hers.

His lips moved, but she couldn't hear anything as he walked her way. She rolled down the window when he reached her door and angled down to lean against it.

"Emmaline Fay, what are you doing? Hiding in the car like a scaredy cat?"

The rich, deep sound of his voice coupled with his childish taunt made her feel self-conscious, and a flush of heat and anger coursed her skin. She'd forgotten about his ability to aggravate her at the drop of a dime.

"No, just trying to decide if this is a good place to park. You know how you country boys tend to scuffle your way over and around cars after a few too many."

"True, but we're men, and we have to impress the ladies somehow. You can't tell me a scuffle doesn't make you smile."

She tried to keep her expression civil even when Jason's familiar scent found her nose, inspiring a fresh round of stomach squirminess. "The only time I feel like smiling is when the cops show up to make an arrest."

Jason grinned. Even his teeth were perfect. Rose had definitely picked a winner. He took a step back and winked. "Come on out of the car, kitty claws. Maybe we can find a scuffle together if you're that excited about the law."

"Always the jokes and nicknames. You haven't changed." She rolled up the window and removed her keys from the ignition. Hilarious how he riled her up and got under her skin with only a few sentences.

15

Keeping her distance should be her key objective of the night. Otherwise she might lean in and sniff him or, worse, engage in one of those arguments she loved to start. *Pathetic.* Maybe her decision to stay out of the dating game was a liability.

She walked to the curb, Jason trailing behind. Glancing over her shoulder, she saw him jerk his head up, and she stumbled on a piece of raised sidewalk.

"Whoa there. Everything okay?" He put a hand to her waist, and she barely kept herself upright.

Her skin went hot. Everywhere. "I'm fine." But she wasn't.

As he pulled his hand away, the once-captain of the football team stared at her butt. Hers. Internal alarms sounded. She couldn't be excited, wouldn't be. He belonged to her best friend. "So...Rose will be here soon."

"I heard. In fact, that's about all I've heard since I got into town. Dad tells me that, besides nursing, she's been busy attempting to get the town some sort of historic status and lobbying for government grants to dismantle Charming Chemical in hopes of drawing people back to this place."

He walked alongside her, and, like a magnet

16

drawn to a metal pole, she wanted to lean in closer. Never in her wildest dreams would she find the courage to ask if he'd experienced the same urge, and, honestly, it was better not to know. The door to Sound Awake stood two feet away. She'd definitely find a place inside to avoid him until his soon-to-be fiancée showed up.

"That's our Rose, intent on saving everyone and everything. She would've made an awesome lobbyist." The thought of the petite prom queen on the steps of Capitol Hill fighting for big causes and small towns everywhere made her grin.

"True, but she could've been anything, and they would've loved her, no matter what. Too bad she believes the town deserves her devotion." He held the door open for her, and, as she walked in, she prepared to be overwhelmed by the smell of stale beer and sweat. Instead, the smell of burgers filled the air, and everything was fine until Jason reached out and wrapped a hand around her wrist. A jolt raced through her, and she jerked back, landing against the bar.

"What's wrong?" he asked.

"Not what I expected." She'd never admit it was the flare of heat he incited when he touched her. It now filled her gut with guilt rather than pleasure. "The bar, I mean."

"New owners have taken over since we were kids, and it definitely looks it." He rubbed his fingers together, eyes on her face. As she'd predicted, his stare possessed the ability to devastate. She searched the room, looking for anything to take her attention away from him—him and his damn soul-searching gaze.

The atmosphere was different here than in city bars with their flashing lights and too-large crowds, the environment more friendly and less concerned with drinking. The patrons, with their small town mentality, concentrated on the gathering.

Her nervousness began to dissipate as she let her hands glide along the dark-stained, smooth surface of the bar. Then she subtly slid away from a certain gorgeous male, refusing to give in to the urge to see if he followed her.

Emma kept moving until she lined up with a face she recognized, a guy behind the bar, pouring drinks. "Hey, bartender, can I get a Bud Light?"

"Coming up, but I'll need to see identification."

She looked the bartender up and down as he grinned at her, all muscle and good looks. His spiked hair reminded her of the urban males she'd often encountered during college. He'd been different when she knew him: quiet, short, and shy, a late bloomer. "Ewan Davis, all grown up and bartending. Wow, you've changed."

He slid an open bottle of Bud in front of her. "For the better, I hope, but you haven't changed at all. Still look as pretty as ever and afraid to admit it. ID?"

She handed him her driver's license and smiled. For some reason, all the boys in Charming were losing their minds, especially if they were attempting to flirt with her. Her mom had said not to pass a good thing by, so she decided to flirt back.

"Hey, why don't you get back to work before I tell your manager you're chatting up the customers," Jason said, sidling in close to her. He was so near, his scent tangled up and around her again. It reminded her of the nights they'd spent swimming by the lake. She and Rose had huddled in close because of the chill. He'd held them both to keep them warm.

She needed to change the subject, change the mood, anything. Thankfully, Ewan did the work for her.

"In most cases, that would be successful, but since I'm the boss, there's no one to report me to."

Em took a long swallow from the bottle, eyes darting between the two men. The looks they exchanged were less than friendly. Prime time for her to take charge. "So, do you hang around with my bestie much? Now, there's a girl to get a number from, Ewan."

"Tried to, but she belongs to Mr. Prince. Always has and always will."

No one would ever forget Jason's once-upon-a-time relationship with Rose Briar. The entire trip had proved exhausting, so far, especially since he couldn't go anywhere without someone mentioning his ex. Comments, questions, and the inevitable, "When are you going to make an honest woman out of her and come back to lead the town?"

Yes, she'd earned the titles of town sweetheart and beauty queen. He'd always be the mayor's son, the golden haired *prince*, but he'd fallen from the pedestal they'd put him on long ago.

He'd also changed, and the town's perfect girl didn't fit what he wanted. No, he wanted...desired...someone else.... That someone stood right next to him. "Yeah, but class separation went away hundreds of years ago. Rose is fair game.

20

You should give yourself a shot."

Every guy in town would've traded their testicles to hear him say those words ten years prior. Regardless of the delay, he'd said them now. How the folks of Charming got hooked on an idea they wouldn't let go of was beyond him.

Then came the death stare. If he'd been watching those green eyes fire up at a guy trying to get her number, he would've been impressed, but Emma was training her famous I-could-kill-you eyes on him. He didn't know how to react, so he threw back a what-the-hell-did-I-do stare.

"I think my friend can decide who she wants to date without any help from you." She tilted the bottle back and took a long pull, finishing the beverage. He couldn't help but glance at her neck and the swallowing movements of her throat. He swelled against his jeans. Surprising what a slender neck and a drink could do to a guy.

"I agree 100 percent. Now can you tell me why everyone is harassing me about her and why you keep mentioning she's going to get here soon?"

"It may have something to do with her being in love with you and planning to win you back," Emma replied, voice laced with annoyance as if she were talking to an idiot. Then she turned toward the bartender. "Would you care to dance?"

"Don't have to ask me twice." Ewan hopped over the bar with ease, hollered at another bartender stationed at the opposite end, and took Em's extended hand.

Okay, maybe he was an idiot some of the time, but the days of prom queen and king were forever gone. The guy fitting those qualifications died his junior year of college. Now he longed to earn some smiles from the one person who believed him capable of more than throwing a football. Except she'd decided to push him away and dance with someone else. His irritation deepened as Ewan twirled the principal's daughter around, and she laughed. A pure, melodic sound. Damn, he needed to figure a way to cut in.

Instead, he got an elbow to his arm from another old school chum standing beside him. "The most beautiful person in the whole wide world just arrived."

Jason tore his focus from Emma in time to see the grand entrance. Today's matched all the others. Rose's long blonde hair swayed, held back from her face with a headband. Her classic heart-shaped face with its set of full, berry-colored lips was capable of igniting wars. A blue top and white skirt showing her shapely legs reminded him of the subtle way she'd always dressed, nothing flashy or skimpy. Eight years ago, he'd have fallen all over himself to be near her, to be the center of her world, but now he found contentment in viewing her as a pleasant memory.

"Hi, Jason." The sweet honey of her voice washed over him. No spell existed any longer.

"Hi, Ro—" She stumbled into him, and he caught her arms just before she would've slid onto the bar floor. "Are you okay?"

"Honey?" The sweet voice that had been laughing moments before now sounded panicky beside him.

This wasn't the way he'd planned the evening. For a second, he wondered if he'd been punked. Her skin felt hotter than popped corn, and her pulse raced underneath the fingers he positioned on her neck. "She's burning up."

He readjusted her in his arms to get a better hold as Emma moved from behind him to put her hands on her friend's face. "You're right. She's on fire. We need to get her to Dr. Mason's. Come on."

As he moved, Rose gripped his shirt. "I'm fine.

Really. No need to worry. Just give me a second. All the excitement of today and you—"

Then she fainted.

"Won't take no for an answer. You're going to the doctor." He gained a good foothold, lifted her up, and rushed out the door, following Emma. He'd make sure she got help; the least he could do for her after everything. Even if she wasn't the woman he planned to be with for the rest of eternity, feelings and friendship never died.

Chapter Two

Because she was unable to undo the wicked wish, but only to soften it, she said, "It shall not be her death."

Emma hammered her fist on Dr. Mason's door. She glanced back at Jason slowly working his way up the sidewalk, Rose limp in his arms. Something was seriously wrong. She knew working with the elderly meant her friend got exposed to all sorts of illnesses, but not any fatal ones at present—at least none that she'd told her about.

"One minute, one minute," came the doctor's bass voice from the behind the door.

"No time, Mason. We've got a sick woman here," Jason shouted back as he reached her. Rose's usual glowing skin was extremely pale and clammy. Emma was praying for a flu bug or exhaustion, easy to combat and treat. The funny part of this whole thing is that the prom queen hadn't been majorly ill since childhood, and she'd maintained a super healthy lifestyle, one she'd been trying to get Em to try out for years.

A lock clicked. The door opened. The doctor, who still sported a bushy mustache, grayed with age, slipped on his glasses and looked out at them. Then he turned on the porch light for good measure. Emma brought a hand up to shield her eyes from the light and the fast influx of bugs.

"Ah, Prince, Emmaline. Who's that you have?" The doc took two steps forward, a frown marring his face. "Come quickly. Place my niece in the examination room. What happened?"

Edging by Em, Jason went first, his steps a quick shuffle. She followed him in, and the doctor slammed the door shut behind them.

"We're not sure," Emma said turning to face the doctor. "She walked into Sound Awake, said about five words, and fainted. When I got to her, she came to for maybe thirty seconds and then fainted again. She's also running a fever."

"Doesn't sound promising. Gladys? Honey, I'm going to need your help," Mason said, walking toward the open door that led to his kitchen. His house had been built onto the back of his office building years ago. Seemed appropriate for the small town doctor who wanted to make sure he was never far from his patients or equipment if he needed to travel out in

26

the night.

Emma followed her friends into the examination room. The smell of laundered linens with a touch of mothballs invaded her nostrils. The scent still surprised her, even after all the time she had spent in labs carrying the same smell.

Rose was already on the table, her arms positioned to rest by her sides. She wasn't moving at all, no tossing or turning, completely unresponsive, except for the slow, labored rise and fall of her chest. Watching Rose like this twisted something in Em's insides, and her hand naturally reached out to swipe away a strand of hair clinging to her friend's lip.

Her motions halted when a female voice called out to her. "Oh, honey! You're finally back."

She turned, only to be embraced by the doc's wife, Gladys. "Sorry I have to see you under these circumstances. It's good to have you home again, dear. I'll slide past you."

"Oh, that's fine." Emma stepped aside.

The petite, white-haired woman, who'd acted as Rose's mother, was also a member of Emma's mother's sewing circle and had played doctor's nurse and midwife until Rose got out of school. As soon as Gladys passed by her, Emma caught Jason's gaze.

"I'll wait out here. Doc says he's going to have to remove a few things," he said, making a circular motion around his clothes.

His decision worked perfectly well for her. She didn't really want him, his tight jeans, or unnaturally good-smelling body to stay. And, of course, a fresh wave of guilt came, thanks to her wayward thoughts. When Rose woke, she'd probably want him, and they could cross that bridge when it arrived. For now, Emma would enjoy the chance to attend her friend without his distraction. "You don't have to wait. I mean, you can, if you want to. I know she'd feel grateful knowing you were here."

His response was interrupted by the sound of metal scraping against metal. Gladys had begun to gather the required patient gown and other equipment to prepare for the doctor's arrival. She gave them both a sheepish smile. "Sorry. Guess I need to break out the WD-40 when we're done here."

He sighed. "I never said anything about leaving, at least not until we know something." Then he walked out, headed for the waiting room.

She refocused on the task at hand, moving to assist the nurse in removing Rose's top and getting a hospital gown on her. Right when she was prepared to help, Dr. Mason entered the room and told her, "You can go ahead and join Jason in the waiting room."

"What? But she needs me. You may need me." She flushed at the mere suggestion she leave. *Where the hell does he get off?* If there was one person less required, Gladys could go, for all she cared. It wasn't like she and Rose hadn't changed in front of each other over the years. Or like she'd never worked with bodies before. Part of her training involved medical work. Chemical engineers had to know how the chemicals they worked with affected the body.

"We're going to draw blood, run plenty of tests and other medical procedures. You'll just end up being in the way and—"

"But I know about medical procedures and proper patient care. I took classes," she responded as reasonably as she could while still cutting the jerk off. So far, Charming's dear doctor had proved to be different than she remembered him. Back then, he'd been nice—eccentric, but nice. Now there were a few choice words she'd use to describe him.

"Classes don't beat experience. Rose is my niece. We'll take good care of her. The best thing you can do is go out there and be patient." *Hardass.*

"But—"

He raised his hand. "No buts. As soon as we have things taken care of, I will let you back in the room. Okay?"

She hated feeling helpless, unable to offer assistance when her friend needed help the most. Not to mention the guilt. If this was karma's way of punishing her for flirting and, truth be told, relishing the look of frustration on the *prince of Charming's* face when she'd left the bar to twirl with Ewan, she'd do what whatever she needed to do to make amends. For now, she'd start by following Dr. Mason's instructions, even if they went against every fiber of her being.

"Fine."

***

Jason looked up from the three-month-old *Sports Illustrated* as Emma walked into the room. Her eyes were red, tears imminent. He didn't have a solution to combat those at the moment, yet he refused to be less of a man by attempting to escape a few waterworks. Sitting up, he raised his arm and motioned for her to come closer. It felt awkward, unlike how he'd been with Rose so many years ago. Emma made him nervous, as if he was afraid he wouldn't measure up. "So what's the verdict?"

She let out a sigh and plopped into the chair next to him. "Nothing yet. Absolutely nothing. They kicked me out of the room, and Dr. Mason said it might take all night to figure things out. Doesn't matter anyway. It's all my fault."

"How?" Jason sat up straight. "You told me yourself it's been three years since you've seen each other. Longer since you left town. If anything, this is probably one of those twenty-four hour super flu bugs. Getting here sooner wouldn't have stopped it."

"I'm her best friend. I should've been here to help. Maybe if I'd offered a little assistance with some of these town projects, she wouldn't be working herself to exhaustion. You really can't say she hasn't been going overboard. What with work, the government grants, the town's historical application...it's too much for one person."

"Yes, but there are other folks in Charming who could play assistant."

Em scoffed. "Really? Because last I heard, there were only a hundred or so, and most of them were either too old or working in multiple positions. The school closed down. The last graduating class got diplomas and left three years ago. I should've stepped up."

"You know, I think you're overreaching here." Jason grabbed hold of her arm for the first time since they had run into each other at Sound Awake. A small jolt traveled through his body as their fingers connected. "I learned a long time ago that I can't be responsible for other people, especially when their dreams and aspirations are different from mine. And you shouldn't regret letting people here follow their own paths. Rose chose her way, and if help was needed, you can bet she'd ask for it."

Her eyes darted back toward the examination room. He couldn't hear anything that gave the impression things were worse than they'd been a few moments ago. In fact, the silence in the room made him anxious, and he started to tap his boot on the linoleum floor. The rising tension around them or the number of feelings invoked knowing someone he cared about lay suffering in the other room failed to help as well. He gave a little shiver and involuntarily gripped Emma's hand tighter. She tried to pull away, but he wanted to hold on to her a little longer.

"All right then, let's break up this mood. I'm

going to read your palm." He hoped the ploy would cast away her urges to break their bond.

"Palm reading?" One brown eyebrow lifted, but her frame and hand relaxed at his touch.

"Yes, I've studied with the finest masters fair corn dogs can buy."

She giggled.

"I can tell you your future, Miss Emmaline Fay," he said with a grin. She gave one back and the effect was breathtaking. She'd always possessed a beautiful smile, one known for lighting up rooms, and he enjoyed being the recipient.

"Fine, Master Prince. Tell me my future."

Jason turned her palm over in his, trailing his fingers along the lines. Leaning in for a closer look, he picked up on the scent of vanilla, flowers, and a hint of something he couldn't identify beyond pure Emma. The power of the smell made his groin swell again, something he didn't need at the moment. One glance downward and she'd see the evidence of how she affected him. So he thought about cold showers and his grandmother's gnarly hands and focused on the soft palm covered with lines.

"Ah, your life line is extremely long. I also see a man in your love line. This is a man who has loved you for a long time and watched you from afar."

She scoffed. "Sounds kind of creepy. I don't know if I want a stalker in my life."

"Not a stalker, but an admirer. He's always appreciated your loyalty." Jason locked eyes with her green ones. "Your kindness and bravery, too. And your ability to push ahead. Strength like that is rare."

She leaned forward, her nose barely touching his. "How rare?"

"Uh." His words caught in his throat. To have her so close, too close...exactly where he'd wanted her since he'd seen her sitting behind the wheel of her car. "Rare enough that I've only known one other person to possess it. I—"

"The fever is coming down," Dr. Mason announced, bursting into the room, face filled with relief.

Jason silently swore as she jumped out of her chair and moved toward the entry. "Can we go in?"

"No, not yet. I want you both to stay here, though, in case you come down with the same thing due to proximity. We've taken blood, and we're doing everything we can, but I don't know if this is contagious." The doctor moved to a cabinet on the far wall and removed two blankets. "You can camp out in the waiting room."

"Completely understandable, Doc. I know we won't leave until Rose is able to, anyway. We'll want to be on the nurse-Rose-back-to-health team." Jason stood to accept the blankets.

Her momentary excitement deflated, Emma shuffled back to her chair. "That's right. I'll be nursing our girl back to health or whatever else it takes, so I'm staying until everything is perfectly fine."

"Good. I'll see you both in the morning," Dr. Mason said, leaving by way of the kitchen door. Jason could only imagine the amount of coffee the doctor planned on consuming for the night.

Emma curled up in her seat, slipping her feet out of her brown cowboy boots.

Jason sat down next to her and leaned back in his chair. "He certainly knows how to offer comfortable beds."

"And there's the sarcasm I know so well." She leaned her head on his shoulder.

He tried to ignore how right it felt. "Yes, and that's why you should just close your eyes and rest. Don't worry. It'll all be better in the morning."

He allowed himself to relax against the high back

of the chair, and Emma stayed in position instead of falling further against his body. Her hair touched his neck, and he longed to reach up and run his hands through it, to see if the long strands were as soft as they'd been years ago. She seemed unable to recognize his feelings for her, but he wouldn't rush her. There was time, even if she guessed at his intentions but didn't want to acknowledge them. Instead, he closed his eyes, too, with a silent prayer that his words promising a better morning would ring true.

Chapter Three

But scarcely had she touched it before the prophecy was fulfilled, and she fell down, lifeless, on the ground.

Emmaline opened her eyes. Everything looked a bit fuzzy.

Then the memory of being at Dr. Mason's house came back full force, including the realization she'd spent all night in a chair and now had a male arm wrapped snugly against her as if attempting to bring her comfort.

Jason. The last thing she remembered, her head had collided onto his shoulder with ease. Obviously, they'd both gotten more comfortable with one blanket on the armrests between them as a cushion and another wrapped around her waist. His breath rustled a few strands of her hair, and the rise and fall of his chest against her arm made the entire moment seem like a dream turned reality. She swallowed, hoping he couldn't hear her throat contracting or the thundering beat of her heart.

"Good morning."

Shit! No time to avoid the awkwardness of the moment. "Good morning." As she began to move, he pulled his arm away. The temperature in the room dropped with the lack of physical contact, and she missed the heat. "Sorry for invading your space last night."

He smiled. "No problem. I—"

"We should probably go check on Rose." Launching up from the chair, she made a beeline for the door, trying to keep him from finishing his sentence. Whatever he had to say would be better off left unsaid. Jason belonged to her friend. That was fate, destiny, and no matter how much she wished the tables turned in her favor, she wouldn't try to change things. His hand slipped around her wrist.

"Stop. There's no reason to rush off yet. Dr. Mason would've told us if she woke up. But I think we need to talk." He'd replaced the smile he'd worn earlier with a frown and something she vaguely recognized as longing in his eyes.

She scoffed. "I don't think we do. Let go of me. Please."

He released her as if touching her suddenly burned. "Sorry, but I need to know. Did you write all those letters after I blew my knee out?"

His question made her legs go weak. There were some letters, but she wouldn't admit to writing them. She'd written out of sympathy, hoping to be an encouragement for him from far away, just like Rose had proved encouragement in person. His football career had been everything to him, and, maybe, deep down, she'd meant more by those notes, but they'd never hold a candle to his high school sweetheart's declarations. In truth, she didn't get the point of the question. Letters or no letters—why did it matter?

She turned away, gathering her strength and assuming her best poker face. When her eyes finally met his, she said, "I don't know what you're talking about."

"You're a horrible liar, Emma. Or should I just call you Fay?"

"That's my last name, so you can call me by either. Now, can we go see Rose?"

He smirked. "Always the smartass. Seriously, switching using your last name as a first name took out any guesswork. Why didn't you ever tell me before?"

The game was up, and she didn't want to admit the truth. She loved him or at least had been in love with a form of him. Regardless of the dormant feelings stirring inside her, this was no time for romantic emotions and trysts that could disrupt her best friend's future, whether he wanted to see it or not.

"I really.... Can we do this later?" *Like never?*

He moved closer, trailing the shape of her cheek with his fingers, his gaze filled with intent, and she sensed one of her daydreams coming to reality. Factions warred within, to pull away or not. She didn't want to, and she was weak, so weak to desire— the looks and the closeness.

"Waiting isn't really my—"

"Emmaline. Jason. Come quick!" Dr. Mason's voice rang out from the examination room.

She ran to the entrance and heard Jason behind her. Inside, the lights were dimmed. Rose's breath came out labored and raspy, her skin as red as the Iowan barns. Her face was flushed, sweat clinging to it, and her eyes closed.

"The fever was going down, and she came to about five minutes ago, but it's come back with a vengeance. She's getting weaker."

Emma looked rapidly from her friend to the doctor and the man who wanted more honesty than she was capable of at the moment. A feeling of futility surged within her, and before she could stop it, a laugh of disbelief forced its way out. "What are you saying? Antibiotics? Air lift? Anything?"

"Emma." Dr. Mason grabbed her hand like an adult coddling a toddler who'd skinned her knee. "I think it's too late for any of that. All my tests come back negative, we've already treated her with ice baths twice overnight, and her fever is over one 107 and climbing. We can't get it down. Her brain cells are burning, and even if the fever disappeared, I don't think she'd be the same. As for air flight, there's nothing available. I've called multiple times. A big crash in Des Moines has called away all helicopters. We're on our own here."

"No!" She yanked her hand away from the doctor and got closer to the bed.

"Wait! I wouldn't get too close. She could still be contagious."

"Screw you, Doc. If this is it, I need to be close." She looked at Jason for support. He seemed distant, eyes only on the most important person in their life. Her ragged breathing was the only sound for what seemed like minutes.

"She's right. Close is what we need now."

"All right. Just no physical interaction, and, for

your own safety, you're wearing surgical masks." The doctor opened a drawer and pulled out two basic powder-blue masks. He handed them over and watched as they put them on. Once the masks were secure, he said, "I'm going for another cup of coffee. I'll be back in two."

"Rose, honey? We're here. Me and Jason." She scanned her friend's face for any recognition, but received no response, just more labored breathing. The whole situation was a nightmare, something out of a soap opera. She'd thought closer would give closure. Instead, a nauseating dread had taken over her body, coupled with helplessness. Plus, she'd been moments away from lip locking with her crush not more than five minutes prior while her best friend lay here dying. "This has got to be the worst dream ever."

"Sure seems like it should be a dream, but it's not. We can't squander this time." He put a hand on her shoulder and moved her to the side. "Baby, you were the best person I've ever known. I was honored to be one of your friends. If I could change places with you, I would, but I bet you'll light up the room wherever you go."

Tears filled Emma's eyes, and she sniffled. "Oh, no. Not yet." He embraced her, arms wrapping around her tight. She rested her head against his shoulder, looking at her friend. "I can't say good-bye. I don't know how." The words came out choked, her throat seizing up at the thought that this would be the last time she'd see her friend. Then Rose's eyes opened.

"Em?" Her question came out on a cough.

She tried to pull out of Jason's embrace and push him aside. Her friend was awake. "I'm here, I'm here." Struggling, she tried to get next to her childhood companion. "Let me go."

"No, you can't get too close. She wouldn't want the same thing to happen to you," Jason said, clenching his arms down to stop her from fighting. She didn't really care. Life wouldn't be the same without Rose in it. The girl had been her supporter, her personal cheerleader, for every moment. They'd been determined to grow old together and have daughters who became best friends.

"He's right." Her friend's agreement was hoarse and croaky. Emma stopped struggling. Even in the worst possible situation, the town beauty thought of someone besides herself. "I'm sorry.... No pillow fight."

Em's tears fell anew, and she sagged, her full

weight pulling against the arms holding her up. "You can't leave me. Not yet."

"I...love you." This time, when Rose's eyes closed, Emma felt a surge of adrenaline. She refused to let go without a fight. She'd soak her in ice for hours if she had to. They couldn't stop her. Her efforts to get her protector to release her bombed as she jammed her shoulders against him with no luck. The attempt to throw her weight around seemed futile, especially since he'd failed to budge an inch.

"Stop," Jason pleaded.

"Please take her out of the room. We'll keep working," Dr. Mason's voice cut through the fog of her fury. The doctor, head bowed over a clipboard, scribbled away furiously, and his wife muffled her sobs with tissues.

Jason started edging in the direction of the door, and Emma let her body slump again, hoping the additional weight would stop him. "Please." The pain in his voice was the determining factor in her suddenly straightening and walking out the door. She didn't look back again, afraid she'd be incapable of stopping her tears if they got going.

***

"Yes, Mr. Fay. Definitely terminal, but Dr. Mason won't tell us anything else. I'll tell him to call you." Jason glanced over at Emma slumped in the waiting room chair. Tissues against her eyes, she'd tried so hard to stop crying, but the tears showed no sign of abating.

"I'll stay with her until then. Yes, sir." He closed the phone and put it back in his pocket. "Your parents said they'll be here within the hour. They went a couple of towns over to pick up a part for the washing machine."

Sniffling, she raised her head. "They probably thought I was with Rose all night. No worriers in the Fay family."

The girl had been damn near heroic, sitting in this room waiting for bad news, the worst news. He didn't know where the courage and love came from. Her grief hit hard, but moments like this, when she emerged from the pain still aware of what was happening, made his heart clench. He wanted to be more to her, a tower of strength she could lean against, but back in the examining room, he'd been a curse. He'd kept her from getting close to the one person with whom she'd spent the most time, the sister of her heart. Losing Rose.... In a word, brutal. He'd loved her as a friend, someone to admire, but if he lost Emma, too, it'd kill him. He didn't need another push back to the dark side.

"What do you need? What can I do?"

"You're doing it. Being here; that's enough. It proves you still love her." She dragged a hand through her hair. Yes, he did, but didn't she realize he loved her, too? He'd fallen in love with the woman who'd told him to become more than a football player, more than the guaranteed future mayor of Charming. She'd been the inspiration that had kept him away from the pills. He had to tell her. This situation proved his earlier thoughts about having plenty of time were crap.

"Em—"

"Just thought," Dr. Mason paused, clearing his throat, "I'd let you both know she's gone. As of five minutes ago. We did everything, but the fever peaked at one hundred and fifteen, and we lost her. Her brain swelled to a point—" The man's tears flowed freely. Eyes puffy, he moved to grab a handkerchief from his coat. "I'll conduct an autopsy on Monday to be sure. For right now, we'll store her. She always wished to be cremated; didn't like the idea of taking up ground space."

"I can't.... Right now, Doc, I can't...." His heroic girl jumped up out of her chair. "Jason, could you take me home?"

He didn't know what to say. Moisture welled in his own eyes. He hated crying. "Yes, I can," he whispered.

"Wait just one minute." Mason walked over and stopped in front of them, applying a palm to each of their foreheads. "Both of you feel all right?"

Jason nodded, along with Emma.

"Then you can leave, but if either of you start getting a fever, feeling nauseated, I want you back here straight away."

"We can do that." Jason spoke before Em did, and shook Mason's hand. "Thank you, Doctor, for everything."

He followed her out the front door, taking one last look at the devastated doctor. The man wasn't known for losing patients, and those who did die in Charming passed in their sleep of old age. This same man had birthed everyone in his graduating class. *Hell.* Now one of those wouldn't get a chance to celebrate her tenth year since becoming an adult. His high school reunion weekend had turned into a tragedy.

***

Emma's body had gone numb somewhere between the ride from Mason's and unlocking the front door of her parents' house. She stood there for a moment, noticing how no birds sang out the songs of the morning, tree branches hung a bit lower, and the grass looked less vibrant. Stumbling inside, she dropped her purse on the entryway table. Jason followed her, chatting on the phone with Ewan, instructing him to take her car back to the driveway. He didn't trust her to drive for the time being. She'd asked for the escort, but, in reality, she wanted to be alone.

Once he hung up, he shut the door. "Are you all right?" He trailed after her into the kitchen.

She grabbed a bowl from the cabinet and headed to the pantry entrance. The object of her mission—breakfast. Regardless of Rose's passing, her stomach growled continuously, and, whether she wanted to eat or not, food had become necessity.

"Fine. I just need some time."

He eyed the cereal box in her hand and moved to

the refrigerator. "That's understandable, but I can help. Or, at least, I'd like too." He placed the gallon of milk on the table next to her bowl. She set the knockoff Lucky Charms down and looked at him. Even with a small shadow of facial hair covering his chin, he was gorgeous, but she couldn't deal with these feelings right now either.

"You can help. Go home, and get some rest."

"But—"

She put her hand on his arm, ignoring the flush of heat accompanying the contact. "No buts. You're exhausted. I'm exhausted. I like the offer of help, but I can't deal with this—whatever this is—between us."

He sighed and moved away. The touching thing— totally her fault, but she couldn't help it. Instead of walking away, he brought one palm to her cheek, and the tears welled again. This tender moment should've been Rose's, not hers, and she didn't deserve it.

"No. Please, no."

Abruptly, his hand pulled away, eyes filled with hurt. "If that's what you'd prefer. I'll catch up with you later." His boots echoed down the hallway, and a few seconds later, the front door shut.

She let the tears fall, cascading down her cheeks

and soaking the collar of her shirt, her brain filled with too many emotions— desire, remorse, guilt, sadness.... The list went on, and she couldn't decide which thought process to sort through first. She collapsed into the closest kitchen chair and put her head to the table. That's when it hit her. *What would my soul sister do?*

She probably would've cried then busied herself with anything and everything. What Emma really wanted was to remind everyone how much they'd miss her, how much she'd done for them. She decided to hold the service this weekend while everyone was in town for the reunion. Besides, the celebration would end as soon as the news spread. How did they celebrate without 'Most Popular'?

Emma jumped up from her chair and grabbed the cordless phone from the wall. A plan began to form in her mind. Phone calls first and breakfast after. Jason and their thing could wait. Rose didn't have the opportunity to wait because, in less than two days, most of the people who knew her best would leave Charming to return to their lives elsewhere.

Her spirits buoyed as she dialed Mrs. Hopkins's number. She'd probably never be forgiven for coveting the man her best friend loved, but she'd at least make sure everyone knew how perfect that same best friend had been in everything she did.

"Honey, where are you?"

Emma stuck her head out of the kitchen door at the sound of her mother's voice. "I'm in here. Just making some phone calls and getting everything squared away. The next part is to get a shower because I look like I slept in a chair all night, which I did. Then I'm headed over to the Briar house."

"Sounds like you've been busy, but maybe you should rest. There'll be plenty of time for everything later." Her mother's hand touched her shoulder, a look of sympathy in her green eyes.

"I'll rest later. Sitting still brings thoughts I can't deal with right now." She turned away to grab her empty bowl and place it in the sink. "Every time I stop moving, my tears start to flow. I've cried enough for now."

Her mom sighed and wrapped her in a hug. She didn't want the closeness or the calming scent of peach perfume. Comfort brought tears, too. The phone calls had been different. With those, distance was available, and all the condolences were easy to dismiss or push aside with little effort. The hug

reminded her of the last loss she'd experienced—
running to her mother's waiting arms with her friend
at her side when the announcement came of Rose's
parents' plane crash.

"It's okay to feel weak, to feel helpless. Grieving
is natural, and if you don't do it—"

She pulled back, staring her mother in the eye. "I
know the importance of grieving, but I don't.... No, I
can't become lifeless because of this. We need to
celebrate and grieve her loss at the same time. With
everyone in town, this is the perfect time to
remember her and her life. I have to do this."

The solution appeared obvious to her, and,
luckily, her mom got the point because her arms
dropped away from Emma's shoulders. She kissed
her on the cheek. "You were always the smart,
realistic one and the best friend a girl could have."

A twinge of guilt hit her. Great best friends didn't
go after their friend's ex-boyfriend. In her defense,
she'd never openly pursued Jason, but, still, they'd
almost kissed. He wanted her, but they'd deal with it
later. Those feelings would have to wait, had to wait.
For Rose. "I'm still trying to be, Mom. I have to go."

***

Jason slammed the door of his car as he got out. Why he'd agreed to show up to help someone who didn't want him or his help still baffled him, but his dad believed the favor was owed out of respect. Walking up the sidewalk, he looked at the house once owned by the "Dry Ice Baron" of Charming. Rose's father had been one of the town's heroes back in the day, starting Charming Chemical and building the quintessential example of what a home should look like. A porch spanned all four sides of a two-story, picturesque country home built the prerequisite six feet from the curb. The beauty queen had inherited it upon her parents' deaths, but had left the house vacant until she'd graduated from high school. This is where he would've ended up if he'd come home after the football debacle instead of staying in Wisconsin.

The front screen door creaked open and, for a split second, he thought his ex would emerge, all dolled up and long legs. Instead, the large frame of Emmaline's father came walking out with a box in his hands.

"Hi, Mr. Fay. Do you need any help with that?"

"Always the respectful young man. You can call me Herb, since you're a lot older now. As for the box,

I think I got this one." He trotted down the porch steps and turned toward the driveway. "Emma could probably use a bit of help in the house, though. She's looking for a few specific things for the memorial tonight."

"Yes, sir." He moved up the steps of the porch, noticing the pair of rocking chairs off to the side. He wondered how many nights Rose had spent on the porch, gazing at the stars.

The teenage pastime was something they'd once enjoyed together, and he knew Emma to be a fan of astronomy as well. Only then did he notice the peeling paint on the siding, and the cracks in the glass on the windows, as if Rose's passing had somehow affected her belongings as much as the people she'd left behind.

Walking into the house, he caught the familiar scent of roses and calla lilies wafting through every room. A peek to the left revealed the living room just as he remembered it the last time he'd been here. It shocked him to see no differences except for the pictures on the fireplace mantel. A few steps closer revealed dozens of photos of their past— summer trips to the lake, campouts, football bonfires, and high school dances. Their prom picture sat front and center, Rose in her creamy white dress and him in his tux. A Ken and Barbie pair.

"I think, deep down, she would've lived those four years over and over again." The sound of Emma's voice jerked him out of his thoughts, and he turned to see her fingering through a small stack of papers.

"I think you might be right, but I can't say I feel the same."

Her eyes snapped to his, and he saw a flash of anger. "Why would you say that?"

"Acne. It was horrible for me those first two years," he replied with a smile. "Especially during football season with that sweaty helmet. Pretty embarrassing, actually."

The anger in her expression melted away, and she let out a small laugh. "True. Can't really escape the *joys* of puberty."

He wanted to say more, but the awkward silence began. Without Rose to direct their interaction in some way, he didn't know how to start all over again. He chuckled at the irony of the situation. Then the laugh turned into a bellyache.

"What's so funny? I mean, puberty isn't the best of times."

"No, it's not that. It's the fact that I can't seem to avoid descending into silence unless we're talking to or about Rose. Even now, she still gets all the attention...although she never really wanted it. You know?"

Her face brightened with a smile, proving he was right. All this time, his ex had dominated their conversations. Every. Single. One. There'd never been room for anything else. He hated the fact that they'd lost Rose, a beacon to the town and one of Emma's support beams, but, without her, maybe he could finally have a chance to know the woman he'd never gotten to know when she'd been a girl.

"You're right. She didn't like being the center of attention, but she knew her beauty and kindness could potentially change the world...so she used it." Em moved further into the room. "I've been a bit dismissive, thinking you didn't really care, but I forget that you two were more than just boyfriend and girlfriend."

"She was my best friend, too. When you weren't together, we were; at least until I left. You know when you were talking last night about letting her down?"

"Yeah. What about it?" She took a couple of steps closer. They were within touching distance, almost too close for him. Could he stop himself from closing the gap?

"Um, well, it's not just your fault." Jason reached out and removed the papers from her hands. "Truthfully, it's my fault, too, if we're assigning blame. We were the closest ones to her, and yet we couldn't bring ourselves back here. I couldn't be the same golden haired 'prince' anymore. And you—"

"What do you mean? This town loved you even when you weren't the football star." She touched his cheek, killing his resolve. As many times as they'd touched in the last twelve hours, it became impossible to control his emotions. She was breathtaking. Those pouting lips demanded attention and that's where he bestowed it, pulling her close and touching her lips with the smallest amount of pressure.

She didn't physically respond except to pull back and inhale a quick breath, "What was that for?"

"For all the times you didn't get a date. For all the kisses you missed. For all the supporting remarks you've given me behind closed doors while being difficult with me in front of everyone. Consider it your reward for loyalty and being the good friend. Now what I can help with?"

"I think I found it." Jason's voice behind her sent shivers down her spine. He'd kissed her, really kissed her. She could still feel the imprint of his lips, the heat behind it, and the desire in his eyes. It'd taken every ounce of strength she retained to pull away from him, to not deepen the first kiss they'd ever shared. Sure, she'd had kisses before— she'd given up holding out a long time ago— yet none of them had put her whole body in some sort of tingling, hyper-aware state.

He expected her to go right back to focusing on the memorial for Rose and figuring out how to get some of her things in order. *Impossible.* Did she feel guilty? *Yes.* She was torn between her body aching for his touch and her mind still determined to keep her from crossing the line. *Could I cross a line if one of the parties was gone?*

Hell, if she'd be able to come up with the answer to that one. Even her mind had started playing traitor, replaying the sensations of that kiss. She moved a paperweight to the side, and then the damn thing went crashing to the floor.

"Fudge."

"Are you okay?" he called, the concern in his

voice apparent.

"Yes. I'm good. What'd you find?" She reached for the clear, flat rock and slapped it onto the table.

Jason came up next to her and handed over a set of papers. "This looks like the information on the historical landmark applications. She wanted to label the town a historic landmark, but was solidifying the proposal down to this house, my parents' house, and the main strip. The property values of the houses aren't super high, but the main strip would be worth any fees."

"How do you know all this stuff about properties and everything?" she asked, thumbing through the papers. The applications were almost complete except for signatures. This whole idea would save the town if it worked and allow it to become more tourist-centric.

"Didn't I tell you? I'm in the realty business, at least the demolition side of things. I can't play sports, but my winning personality does well in that line of work, I guess. My company brings down abandoned, derelict buildings, and being around all the sales guys, architects, and Realtors, I pick up a few things."

"Who knew? Ex-football captain had a future as a realty expert. That's not a far cry from politician."

He held up his hands and backed a few steps away. "No, don't even go there. I don't plan on ever being a politician. The responsibility is too much."

"You never were big on responsibility." She laughed and set the papers down. Trying to locate pictures of good memories with Rose for the slide show so far had proved more difficult than she'd originally thought. "But you've got a right to do what you want to."

"Tell that to my father. He believed I was the future of the town. With Rose at my side, we were going to bring Charming to new heights. Now, his dream is gone."

A sharp twinge of jealousy flew through her. Everyone always assigned them roles, and, just once, she wanted to be assigned to him. Pushing her personal emotions back, she turned to look at him.. Shoulders locked, his frown deepening, he flipped through a few pictures on the table. The expectations he'd mentioned equated to the same ones everyone else in town had, and now she wondered if his father's dream had somehow transferred and instilled itself in the minds of others over the years. "Yes, I guess it is. But today is about Rose's dreams. Not your father's or mine or anyone else's. Let's celebrate hers."

"You're right. I'll keep looking." He turned to leave the room, and she went back to her rummaging. A warm hand grasped her shoulder. "Thanks."

"You're welcome." The heat of his arm left her, and she knew working on this project with him so nearby would be near impossible. Wanting him still felt wrong. And as to the customs regarding dead friends' exes, she didn't play these games, she didn't know the rules, and— desire be damned—she refused to crumble her friend's memory for something unpredictable. How she'd convince Jason that being together would be impossible when he seemed determined to show her otherwise required a level of steadfastness equivalent to that of saint. Yet she didn't need more guilt, and she was pretty sure he didn't need any either.

Chapter Four

However, she was not dead....

Everyone and their mothers, cousins, aunts, and uncles, all one hundred of them, had turned out for the memorial, not to mention nearly the entire visiting senior class and their spouses, a grand total of twenty folks.

In a small town, news didn't stay small for long. Emma's mom and dad had told her when she got home that at least four casseroles and five pies were already in the kitchen, the reward for bearing the mantle of responsibility that came with managing all the funeral arrangements. Cremation and the actual funeral would be several days from now since the Charming funeral home had closed down a few years prior, and all bodies were picked up by a home over two hours away. The mourning treats sat on a table with countless more and a huge punch bowl at the back of the gym. She brushed her hands through her hair.

"Nervous?"

A tingle fell down her spine, and she jerked at the heat radiating from Jason's body.

"I'll take that as a yes," he said with a chuckle.

"You shouldn't sneak up on people."

"Why not? The reaction I get from you is refreshing."

She whirled around to face him. "Refreshing, huh? Well, the reaction I'm having involves a kneecap and a sensitive part of you."

"I like it when you're feisty." He laughed again and snaked his arms around her, pulling her in close.

She saw the look. He planned to kiss her again behind the curtains with the whole town on the other side. What if someone came looking for her? What if her parents saw? Oh, her mother would be over the moon, but still.... She didn't want the questions.

"We can't." She gave his shoulders a shove. "Not here. Not now. Preferably, not ever."

"I know you don't mean that. Not after today."

"Well, I mean it. Time. I need time."

"Fine," he replied, moving off to the side. He peeked out through the curtain. "Looks like you've got a full house, and I just came to let you know the slideshow is ready."

"Em, the sound system is loaded." Ewan's announcement came with his entrance onto the stage. Dressed in black, he'd volunteered to help her with anything. He handed her a small black controller. "This will allow you to turn on the slideshow whenever you're ready, and the second button will trigger the music." He pulled her into a hug and whispered, "I'm sorry for your loss. It's hitting everyone pretty hard, but I know their grief doesn't hold a candle to yours. If you need me, let me know."

"I will, and thanks." She squeezed him hard.

"Hey, Ewan. Your mother told me to pass on the message that she's waiting for you." Jason's words ended their embrace. He slowly let go of her hand and then left. "Thinking of kissing him next?"

She didn't miss the jealousy in his statement. "Does it matter if I do?"

No sense in looking at him, especially when the pain in his eyes would be too much to bear. She was wrong to taunt him with Ewan, especially since the bartender's embrace caused no reaction beyond comfort. No heat, no prickling, or goose bumps like the ones that arose anytime Jason got near. As she began to part the curtains, he uttered near her ear, "We both loved her, you know. That doesn't mean I should be punished for wanting you, too."

Stepping through the curtains, heart pounding in

her chest, her mind seemed to be splitting in two. She wanted to comfort him, admit her own feelings, but Rose came before them, before anyone else. If not, then what kind of friend could Emma call herself?

A bright light flooded the stage, breaking her focus. After a few seconds of squinting, her eyes adjusted. She could see most of the crowd. Her parents, Dr. Mason, Gladys, and Mrs. Hopkins filled up the first row. Other town council members were close to the front, too. The stomach jitters took over, and she remembered how much she despised public speaking. *Too late now.*

"Hi, everyone—" She cleared her throat and started again. "I mean.... Hello, Charming High Alumnae and everyone who turned out for what we'd intended to be our tenth year reunion. This occasion has now become a tragic moment for all of us." Pausing, she glanced down at her notes on the podium, attempting to gather strength amidst the sniffles, sounds of chairs scraping along the gym floor, and muffled sobs. Then she caught sight of a figure toward the back of the gymnasium. It looked an awful lot like Rose from far away; her cheerleader there in spirit.

"Rose Briar was the best of us, the beacon of light

for this dwindling town. She, like her father before her, put the town of Charming on her list of responsibilities and was determined to bring us into the next century. She had a ton of plans, which included historic landmark status as well as removing the old chemical factory to ensure the town's safety."

Em glanced back at the spirit of Rose, or at least what she had thought was her spirit. The figure slowly stumbled forward, moving farther into the room. "But there was more to our reigning homecoming queen than saving everyone and everything. Her life inspired kindness and a true beauty. To share those memories, I have a slide—"

"It can't be."

The exclamation from one crowd member was followed up quickly by another. "That's her."

She looked again at the person she'd mistaken for her friend's spirit, visible to everyone. The floodlight on the stage disappeared, and the lights in the gym came on. Between the rows stood her friend, eyes dark and bloodshot, skin pale. Em's mouth parted, and she wanted to go to her but couldn't move. *You're alive.*

Sheriff Fowler and Dr. Mason moved from their chairs and began to approach Rose, arms outstretched in a tentative manner.

"Sweetie, it's us. I'm going to come closer to help you." Mason reached for her arm, and Emma's sickly friend let out a guttural growl, launching herself at the sheriff. Several screams filled the air, and Emma let out a gasp when the sound of torn flesh echoed over the cries. At that sound, the crowd jumped into action. Women and children ran for the door as Ewan, Dr. Mason, and a couple of other men she vaguely remembered grabbed for the wild woman gnawing on the sheriff's shoulder. They pulled her off, and she thrashed about, fighting to free herself. However, with one man on each arm and another holding onto her legs, she couldn't move.

"No! Let her go," Em yelled, running for the stage stairs. Her legs moved faster than her two-inch-heeled feet did, and she almost tripped on the last step. She inhaled sharply, ready to charge, when a strong arm encircled her waist and pulled her back. The only other people left in the gym were a group of men slowly moving her friend toward the door. Ewan remained behind and helped Fowler to his feet.

"You need to release me. They're hurting her."

"We have to get out of here," Jason said into her ear.

Rose howled and ripped her arm free from a deputy, scratching at Ewan's younger brother, Peter, on her left. She was a madwoman, depraved and insane. Nothing like the person they'd known. In fact, this thing was an imposter. Then a popping noise, followed by a squelched and unearthly scream from Peter, filled the gym. Blood spurted into the air, and the creature that looked like Rose wildly sucked on Peter's detached, bloody arm as his body fell to the floor.

Sheriff Fowler drew his gun, yelling, "Freeze! Drop the arm, and get down on the ground."

No response came from the woman continuing her feeding frenzy on the arm in her possession. The other deputies looked on in horror. The sheriff cocked his gun, Rose lifted her head, and *bang!* The shot hit center mass.

"Noooo!" For the second time in a day, Emma sagged into Jason's embrace as she watched her friend's body fall to the floor. This was worse than the fever. She refused to watch any more. Her eyelids closed, horrified by the foulest case of violence this small town had ever experienced. Limbs numb, she could hardly object as her protector lifted her and carried her out of the building.

***

Jason set Emma down long enough to open the door of his car. He coaxed her into the passenger seat, moving as fast as he could while still being gentle. Then, slamming the door shut, he hopped into the driver's side. His ex was alive or something. At least she'd been moving. That concept, he couldn't wrap his head around. Keys in the ignition, he started the car and backed out of the parking lot, determined to remove them from the high school before the guys paraded the dead body out of the gym.

"How? I just—how? Doc declared her legally dead."

"I don't know. You got me, but I'm sure the sheriff and Mason will get the whole thing figured out."

A sigh fell from her lips, but he couldn't take his eyes off the road to offer sympathy. She let out a little laugh. "This is just a nightmare, right? We're both going to wake up tomorrow and realize we've been sleeping through twenty four hours of fake hell. Right? I didn't see my childhood friend eating someone's arm?"

"I can't think about that right now," he replied, pulling into her driveway. "I'll walk you in since it looks like your parents are still out."

The house was dark, but even though he hadn't been in her house in years, he remembered the hallway light switch next to the front door. Flicking it on, he watched Em slip out of her heels, kicking them across the floor toward the staircase. As he locked the front door behind them, a twinge in his gut told him it made sense to play things safe—just like in the big city.

"Thanks for getting me out of there," she said as she walked into the living room.

He followed her, turning on the fan and main light. She'd wandered near the fireplace, still dazed, face swollen from crying.

"No thanks needed. That's what I do. I rescue."

She leaned against the mantel. "Yes, you do, but I think I'm good for now. If I need any additional rescuing, I'll let you know."

"I'll have my white horse at the ready."

He moved closer to her, the smell of her filling him up. Even with tear-stained cheeks, she looked beautiful in her black dress, her hair pulled back from her face. He was good for more than rescuing, especially in the comforting department. And, hell, he needed some comfort, too, after seeing his ex ripping into a pillar of the town as if his arm were a turkey leg.

"Do you think you could take me to Dr. Mason's in the morning?"

"I guess I can, but why don't you just call?"

"It's more than a phone call can deliver. I need closure and to understand. I've got a degree that includes basic medical and biology training. We've got to know how those chemicals you're fooling around with affect people. What happened tonight doesn't make sense." She stood tall now, arms crossed and green eyes sparkling with frustration. In many ways, she acted like Rose, determined to discover the solutions to their problems. Except the ones he wanted her to solve, like how they could expand on the feelings stirred up by their kiss.

"Fine. I'll do it."

He didn't want to, but she'd go alone without him. Something about the whole situation with Rose struck him as off. The horror film mentality aside, he wouldn't mind learning more from the good doctor about Rose's illness and death. He especially wanted to ask why his ex awoke from the dead and how she had removed herself from a body freezer in the doc's basement.

"Emma?" Edy's voice sounded in the main hallway, and, within seconds, Em's father and mother charged into the living room. Jason took a step back, letting Mrs. Fay slide in and wrap her daughter in a hug. "I'm so sorry, honey."

"Jason." Herb gave him a respectful nod.

"Sir. I was just getting ready to say good night."

"No worries there. I'm glad you brought our girl home safe. Your father did wonder where you were. I spoke with him and the sheriff. Doc's patching Fowler up now. Peter, the deputy who lost the arm, died from blood loss."

Em stepped out of her mom's embrace with a worried expression at the mention of the sheriff. "That's awful. Is the sheriff all right?

"All right, but shaken. He just shot the daughter of one of his closest friends, so I can't say he'll feel perfect anytime soon. And losing Peter won't be easy, but we'll see."

Jason could understand the feeling of acting out of character and doing something you were compelled to do versus wanted to do. The memories of the pain, the pills, and the shakes assailed him.

Deciding to leave without announcing his departure, he walked out of the room.

***

Emma tried to close her eyes for the twentieth time, but again came the image of Rose growling, her face contorted like some inhuman snarling animal, and Emma shivered in fear. She needed something, anything, to rid the visual from her mind. The only other thought she'd been able to conjure was Jason's face, a flare of light in his deep, ocean-blue eyes, after the kiss they'd shared in Rose's living room. Her heart began to race, guilt flooding her gut at her selfish desires. Either way, thanks to nightmares or sensual dreams, she wouldn't be sleeping tonight.

Chapter Five

For the princess was so beautiful and well-behaved and amiable and wise that everyone who knew her loved her.

The smell of fresh-brewed coffee propelled Emma, exhausted and fresh from the shower, down the stairs. The hot water she'd emerged from minutes before had barely washed away the first layer of fogginess.

Her nightmarish dreams kept playing over and over; Rose attempting to eat her and ripping her arms to shreds. The images hadn't looked pretty—her friend far worse for wear than the night before, her skin rotted from the bone, arms reaching out. She shook the final thought away as she rounded the corner and entered the kitchen.

"You okay, honey?" Her mom thrust a coffee cup toward her.

She latched onto the cup and inhaled deep. "Uh-huh, as soon as I get this coffee in me." After a few sips, she took a seat at the table, and the synapses began to fire. "Any news on the sheriff?"

Her dad stood at the stove, flipping pancakes,

the smell of warmed maple syrup wafting past her nose. Breakfast in the Fay house could energize a weary army. Her stomach let out a growl, reminding her that the cheese and crackers from the night before had been inadequate.

"I spoke with the mayor around seven this morning. Fowler is down with a fever at Mason's." Her dad placed a plate of pancakes in front of her. Their eyes met, and she could tell whatever he had to say next, she wouldn't be happy about. "Emma...I— No, your mother and I think it's best for you to stay away from the doc's. He still doesn't know what Rose had, but Doc swears she was already gone when you were at his house. There's a bit of a medical mystery around how she could have been up and moving last night."

She shook her head, pissed at them for trying to stop her and even more upset because she knew who'd told them about her plans. "Good reason for me to be there. I'm a biochemical engineer. What if this is something she got exposed to, a weird chemical from the plant or something else?"

"Then you can let someone else take care of it." Her father slammed his hands on the counter. She understood the situation scared him, but, with the sheriff sick, perhaps Rose's illness was catching. The fever and death rattle had obviously been a ruse, the illness forcing her into a state of hibernation. The theoretical possibilities were pinging around her brain by the dozen and at the speed of light.

"I know you want me safe, but I can't stand by and not discover the cause of my friend's death. I need closure. Do you understand that?"

Her dad turned away, shoulders tensed and fists still clenched. She wished he understood her desire to know for the sake of moving on and the sake of forgiving herself for wanting Jason, except she'd never admitted the last little bit to anyone. Plus the need to know operated like some strange curiosity niggling at her brain the same way a complicated chemistry problem would. This whole situation may have been karma for her carrying a secret torch for her friend's ex. Shoving another bite of pancakes into her mouth, she hoped to silence the argument by stuffing her face. A glance at her mom told her she'd get no support from that corner since she'd already edged her way out of the kitchen. Most likely, Edy Fay had initiated the topic of this debate.

"No, I don't understand." *No such luck.*

He turned off the stove and moved to place the

skillet in the sink. "I don't see how you justify putting yourself on the line without thinking about what the other people who care about you are feeling. It's selfish."

"I don't think it's selfish." Recognizing her white knight's voice, she shifted in her seat. Jason stood at the entrance to the kitchen. He looked as exhausted as she did but still gave her a small smile. "Sorry, sir, but I believe your daughter is the exact opposite. I also know the desire for closure and the need to come to terms with the cause of your pain."

Her face flushed. He'd heard every word she said. "What are you doing here?"

"I've been here for an hour or so, sipping coffee in the living room. You said you needed me to take you to Doc's this morning, and your mom said you were almost done with breakfast."

Her own personal polo-and-jean hero, dressed every bit the modern warrior, stood in her doorway, sipping the last of his caffeine and defending her from her father. She wanted to either drool or thank him. Of course, her inner smartass beat all good intentions to the ground. "I didn't mean you had to show up at the crack of dawn."

"True." He took another mouthful of coffee and

swallowed, Adam's apple bobbing with the movement. Clean shaved and everything. *Damn.* "Whenever you're ready."

Her father stayed quiet and scrubbed the pan in the sink. Frustration still lined his face, and a fresh wave of guilt, an ever constant companion these days, washed over Emma. She shoved it aside, resolved to openly defy her father again. The same argument from years ago popped into her head....

"I'm an adult now, Daddy. I can make my own choices."

"Yes, but your choice is wrong."

"I don't think being over five hundred miles away from you is wrong."

She couldn't live in the past, and, in times like these, she trusted her gut. Hiding behind pain and remaining ignorant about the truth didn't fit her nature either. Gut instinct told her solving the mystery remained the best possible choice. A few more fork-loads of pancake, and she'd finished her small stack. "I'm ready."

Putting her plate on the counter next to the sink, she gathered her strength, leaned up on her tiptoes, and kissed her dad on the cheek. "I know you think I make all the wrong decisions, that I do things just for me, but something tells me stepping up to the plate this time is different. This is about all of us. I feel it. Regardless, I love you no matter what."

She turned away and headed for the door. There was no reason to look back and see the effect her words had wrought no reason to dwell. "I'll be in the car," she said, passing Jason and exiting the room. Maybe her dad could forgive her at some point for taking her own path.

"She's the most stubborn creature I've ever met," Herb said with a shake of his head as Jason set his empty coffee cup on top of Emma's plate. "You'll keep her safe for me?"

Jason lifted his head from the *Charmed in Charming* coffee cup to stare Herb in the eye. *How do I convey the word's 'with my life' to a father?* He could've said them, but such a declaration meant admitting to a depth of feeling that might not be reciprocated. So, instead, he swallowed the last of the coffee in his mouth and replied, "To the best of my ability, sir."

"Respectful and straightforward. I like this grown-up version of you, prince." Em's dad slapped his shoulder with a soapy hand. "Don't let her give you any grief. I'll let you get going."

Grief.... Let's hope we don't experience any more.

Jason walked out of the house, dragging his sunglasses into place from their perch on the top of his head. Emma sat in the passenger seat of his car. The sun gave a glow to her hair, a fine contrast to her creamy, flawless skin. Though her puffy eyes remained, he found them part of her allure, part of her character. The image stunned him, and he silently wished he could bottle up the momentarily peaceful look on her face as their eyes met. She seemed equally appreciative of his appearance, giving him a shy smile.

"Are you smiling for someone special, or is that a natural reaction to seeing me?" he asked.

Her eyebrows scrunched down. The beaming look disappeared. "Ooh, why do you have to do that?"

"Do what?" he asked, sliding into the driver's seat.

"The thing where you make some arrogant comment or cheesy pick-up line. Really? I thought you were better than that." Her voice dripped with sarcasm as she tried to change the mood, to avoid the moment...again.

He whirled on her, removing his sunglasses and running his eyes over the course of her entire body. Delectable. The only word to describe what he saw. Except they didn't have time for him to give her a detailed account of how she affected him since they needed to get a move on. She shivered. His scrutiny was causing a reaction.

"Then let's get real." He ran a single finger down her cheek and across her lips. "I've wanted to be close to you for longer than you can imagine. Seeing you again has been my goal this entire trip. Is that better?"

"Uh...." Emma's eyes darted back and forth, desperate to avoid him, but unable to. That jade green gaze finally settled on him.

"That feeling you have right now, the desire, the guilt. I feel all those things, too. But not in the same way. It's like I'm pushing you, grappling against an unseen force for the smallest bit of acknowledgement or affection when I want to give you so. Much. More."

He leaned in to place a feather-light kiss on her lips, and she moaned. The pull to rush, head first, into kissing her with all the intensity he wanted to stood a hair's breadth from being released. Her face flushed red, eyes closed, as her body leaned into him.

She would've been joy in his arms, and the urge to throw caution to the wind and claim more of her, right there in front of her parents' house, proved damn tempting until he saw the flutter of white lace curtains at the living room window. Instead, he started the car and pulled his sunglasses back in place.

"Who are you?" Em asked. She leaned back in the seat and secured her seatbelt, confusion etched on her face and her cheeks still in high color. *An attractive look on her.* A smug grin overtook him along with a sense of pride in knowing he could fluster her thoughts.

He carefully backed the car out of her parents' driveway, checking the mirrors multiple times. "Just a Prince," he replied, smiling big.

***

Emma knocked on Mason's door and waited. Jason stood beside her, looking around at the windows, the sheriff's car in the driveway, and at generally everything except her.

She felt a bit awkward and giddy. Jason Prince wanted her. The idea seemed unreal, but the way he'd phrased the whole ordeal was unlike any other guy who'd taken an interest in her. If he'd kissed her again, she would've given in like a kitten, weak and desperate for someone to stroke it.

Damn him for wanting more. He cared for Rose, but not in the way he wanted her. Was he guilty of a bigger sin? Could she really convict him when his confession hadn't solely involved lust or sex?

"What's wrong?" he asked with a frown. He pounded on the door with a closed fist.

"Nothing. Just thinking things."

"Like?" The look in his eyes said he didn't want her to regret his words. She wanted to be involved, be close, which gave her equal hot and horrible emotions all over.

She leaned up to peek through the glass, but couldn't really see anything. "I wonder where everyone is." The other strange thing she didn't want to mention was that the grass was dead; a browned, shriveled-up dead. In fact, all the flowers in front of the Mason's place were decaying, too.

"Don't know, but the clinic should be open. So—" He turned the knob and opened the door. "Let's go in and see if we can get an appointment. After you."

He bowed at the waist and extended his arm. She

stepped into the building, and a pang of heartache hit hard as she remembered the millions of times his deferring mannerisms had gone to Rose and not her. They both entered the waiting room, which was empty. No Doc, no sheriff, no Gladys.

"Doc?" she called out, taking slow, measured steps through the room. If the doctor had left, there would've been a sign on the front door, so where were they?

She switched on the light in the examination room. As the fluorescent tubes emerged from slumber, she expected to see a sleeping Sheriff Fowler in bed, but nothing. In fact, no evidence of a patient existed in the room. The little refrigerator on the counter caught her eye, though. Especially the vials of blood labeled "Rose Briar"; the next best thing to the autopsy report. "Jason, where are you?"

"I'm right here," he said from behind her. "It's too quiet. I'm going to see if anyone is at the back of the house. Maybe eating breakfast or something."

"Okay. I'll see if I can find the notes on Rose." She moved further into the room, glancing over the contents and hoping to locate the file cabinet.

"Shouldn't you wait and talk to him?"

"Think about it. Why would he tell me anything?

He already thinks I wasn't much help anyway. It won't hurt to look either. I mean he won't have me locked up for looking at a file. Bingo." A tan-colored, two-door cabinet sat on the other side of the bed behind the curtain.

"Fine. I'll be back, but if you hear me talking to him, I'd put whatever you're into away and get out to the waiting room fast."

"Sure thing." She opened the top drawer and started skimming the folder names. Everything filed away in alphabetical order. *Thank you, Gladys.* Not to be down on the dear doctor, but she'd seen his handwriting before and his office. Gladys kept everything organized from the house to the examination rooms. Halfway through the drawer, she located the folder she needed. She hefted the monstrosity out. All the files were that large since most of the high school alumnae had been born in this very room. Emma set the file on the counter and flipped to the back half of the paperwork, eyes skimming over each page.

Finally, she found examination notes from the day before. The fever was listed as 'cause unknown.' Blood work and initial tests had come back negative for common flu, viral infections, and drugs. The other tests were inconclusive. And no sign of the autopsy report.

"Damn." They probably kept those files in the basement morgue, and no amount of curiosity could get her down into that dark, dank room. *Nope.* Knowing somebody died and wanting to find the cause was one thing. Signing up to glimpse her dead body cut open rested firmly in the category of things Emma wanted to avoid. She moved to the refrigerator and stared down at the vials of blood. No time to do any digging, nor did she have the proper equipment, but if she took a vial for later, it couldn't hurt.

But it's stealing.

Her options were slim, and, ethically, glancing over files equated to an invasion of privacy. Now she wanted to add stealing vials of blood, which could warrant a call to the sheriff's office. *Screw it.*

She was opening the refrigerator door when Jason rushed into the room. "We have to go. Now."

"Just give me one second. I'm going to find something to put this in." She reached out to grab a vial.

"No." He grabbed her arm and pulled her away from the fridge. "There's no time."

She couldn't do anything but follow as he nearly

dragged her out of the room. He didn't care about the lights, the open fridge, or the files. As they set a brisk pace, the only thing she could think was that it had something to do with the strange smell she'd picked up as they went through the waiting room. Once outside, she twisted from his grasp. "What the hell are you doing? I nearly had a way to get answers to Rose's sudden recovery."

"Just get in the car."

She stood still, arms on her hips. His demands could take a flying leap. He walked over to her, took her by the elbow, and pulled her toward the car. Never one to simply give in, she tugged back, circled her arm around, breaking his hold, and then shoved him away. "'Caveman' doesn't work with me."

He growled in response, "I'll explain when you get in the car."

They faced off for a few more moments, and, finally she got in, slamming the door shut. *What a jerk!* The whole thing reminded her of being five years-old, and, like then, she ached to throw the mother of all tantrums unless he explained things fast. In a matter of seconds, Jason had started the car and peeled down the street. Something had gotten him all impatient.

"Can you explain things now?"

Jason kept his focus on the road as he took a few deep, calming breaths. His hands shook on the wheel, and his face was pale. "Give me minute."

"No more minutes. I was in the middle of something when you barged in, acting all crazy and hauling me out of there. What gives?" she asked, throwing her hands in the air.

"What gives is two dead bodies, Doc and Gladys, with parts hanging out."

A chill stole over Emma, and her arms broke out in gooseflesh. "What do you mean? How? Who?"

"I don't know. But my best guess is that Sheriff Fowler went nuts. I checked the basement. Rose isn't there either, so your guess is as good as mine as to where her body up and went." He ran a hand through his hair.

Emma was shaken. Her throat tightening, she tugged on a strand of hair until the pain receptors on her scalp fired off. Another reality check, a reminder all the insanity around them was truly happening. A closer examination of Jason's clammy, sweat-beaded forehead told her he was barely holding it together. Yet he'd held up better than she would've. Dead bodies, in theory, were fine to study. In reality, she'd kept to lab specimens that held no personal sway over her own emotions. Seeing people you had loved, known, all your life, not merely dead, but maimed...different story. There were no words to make the moment right, no solutions in her mind. If people were going nuts and attacking each other, was Rose the cause? How did a person who had died twice come back again? The million dollar question.

Chapter Six

Then the twelfth, who had not yet given her gift, came forward and said that the bad wish must be fulfilled....

"We can't just sit by and do nothing. This is Rose, our friend," Emma said as Jason pulled into said friend's driveway. Why he had returned to an empty house with nothing but memories, she didn't know. There were better locations to go to, including her parents' house, but she'd been too stunned to say so. "Why are we here?"

"I don't know." He slammed his hands against the steering wheel before waving them around in the air. "Clues, maybe? She wasn't feverish and near death's door two days ago. What happened? It's Saturday. She died Friday morning. If we want to save her and anyone else, we have to know more about what they've got." Shaking his head, he pulled the keys from the ignition and got out of the car.

She shut the door to the Mustang and sprinted toward the front door. "Okay, so clues. I spoke to her a couple of times on the way into town. Everything sounded normal for her; she even dropped the phone once."

They stepped into the front hallway, and she scrutinized the room, willing the answers to their questions to magically appear in front of them. His points made sense, but she wanted desperately to rewind the clock, to get a chance to warn her friend and even herself. And then she remembered something.

"Hey, remember the senior carnival?"

"Yes, but what does the carnival have to do with two people going on a cannibalistic killing spree?" He stepped into the living room, rifling through a pair of jackets draped on the back of the couch.

"It has a lot to do with it. Remember the fortune teller? She said Rose would get sick or something in ten years."

Jason turned, locking his fear-clouded, wide eyes with hers while biting his lower lip. "No, she said she'd release a sickness." He picked up the picture of both of them at the prom, and rubbed his thumb over his ex's face. "Don't tell me this is what that lady meant."

She shrugged. "It might be, but I hope not."

Just thinking of that strange woman gave Emma chills.

"Okay, so we need to track down the fortune teller. Didn't she work at the school as a janitor or something?"

"So you do remember more about those days." She let out a small smile.

He had always pretended to be so uninvolved back then, making everything a joke, when, truthfully, he had absorbed plenty of details. Placing the picture back on the mantel, she failed to stop the sigh escaping her lips, nor the appreciation she had for him, which ran deeper the longer they spent time together.

"Yeah, I remember. Quit looking at me like that. You can't deal with the feelings between us right now, remember?"

"Sorry. Couldn't help it." Her momentary admiration disappeared, his words like a knife slicing through her. "Like you couldn't help kissing me in the car earlier." She'd love to forget all their troubles and melt into something hot and wonderful, but she'd never been the type to let her passions rule her. More with Jason would mean just that—more. At the moment, it didn't seem right to want more, but it didn't mean she couldn't move in that direction—at a slow, respectful pace.

She shook her head to clear away the idea of getting into this conversation again, even though she'd involuntarily egged it on. "Forget I said that."

"Fine. I will." His abrupt tone put the nail on the feelings coffin for the moment.

"All right then. Mrs. Wiggs, janitor hired during our senior year. I always thought she was creepy because she had really long nails. Witchy nails."

He laughed. "Long nails? That could be said for half of the old ladies in Charming. Let's focus on bigger details. Where did she live?"

Why did he have to look so great when he laughed? And why did their weekend have to be destroyed with such devastation?

"Emma? What are you thinking about?" He snapped his fingers in front of her face. She shook her head again and felt a pull in her gut. There wasn't a person out there, besides Rose, that she'd rather face all this crap with than Jason. They needed to solve the problem and keep themselves safe because she wouldn't lose him, too.

"We really need to figure out where this lady lives."

"Yeah, Mrs. Wiggs. Let me call my dad." She pulled her phone from her pants pocket. He moved deeper into the living room while she dialed and then disappeared from her line of sight just as her father picked up on the other end of the line.

"Hey, Dad."

"Honey, where are you? I got a call from Mrs. Hopkins a few minutes ago, saying she saw Sheriff Fowler attack his son."

Things were worse than she thought— way worse. "I'm at Rose's house with Jason. We're fine. About that—"

"Okay, stay where you are, then. I've already called the mayor, and we're rounding up the other deputies to track down the Fowlers."

Her throat went dry at the idea of her father and the mayor sending deputies to hunt down the sheriff of their town for the last forty years along with his son. She opened her mouth to form words, cognizant of the fact that her father's voice droned on, and then broke for a few seconds to speak with her mother. Nightmare, horror film—this rated as worse than both.

"Dad."

"What, honey? Your mother just wanted to know if you're safe."

She sighed. "I'm fine, really. You need to know....

Doc Mason and his wife are dead. Jason found the bodies when we stopped by there."

Silence was the response followed by whispers and her mother's sobs. Her mother's sewing circle had officially lost one of its founding members. This made everything more difficult. In a big city, there existed a certain anonymity in death. In a small town, each death left a hole in your heart, her parents' reactions being far worse than her own since they knew everyone more intimately than she did.

"Dad?"

"Yes, I'm still here." His voice choked as the words came out.

"Remember Mrs. Wiggs?" She really hoped he did because if the woman had predicted the disaster, she could predict a solution.

"You mean the janitor from the high school?"

"Yes," she said, dropping her shoulders in exasperation. Her mother's sobs became clearer in the background. "Do you know where she lives?"

"I think she lives out behind the factory near the top of Mount Charming. Liked the quiet life away from town. I'm going to head out in a bit to assist the mayor or at least see what I can do to get Mrs. Hopkins to come stay with us."

She put her free hand to her head, massaging her temples. The idea of her father putting himself in danger in such a way scared her, but she couldn't argue against him, especially when he'd been unable to stop her from helping out. No, his mind, once decided, didn't stray from a decision.

"Be careful."

"You, too, sweetie, but why are you trying to find Mrs. Wiggs?"

The question made her pause. She slapped her forehead. This story would be best told at some other time. Besides, how did you explain that an old woman who scrubbed bathroom floors predicted this fiasco years before? She decided to leave things up in the air rather than dig herself into a deeper pit of stink.

"Jason thinks she may be able to tell us something. Maybe this whole thing is chemical or drug related."

"Okay. He's not involved in drugs, is he?"

"Not really the time for me to ask him, but seriously— we're talking about Jason here."

"Right, fine. Fine. Just be careful going out there."

"Sure. I love you. Bye," The last word came out

halted by the knot forming in her throat. The idea of her father being brought down by a psychotic sheriff and her never getting to make up for this morning's arguments made rounds inside her head.

"Love you, too, sweetie." When he hung up, she stuck the phone back in her pocket.

Jason's eyes were sad, focusing on her like he'd stripped away any barriers and left her mentally naked. "What's wrong?"

"The sheriff attacked his son. Things are getting worse." Vulnerability and grief weren't emotions she usually dealt with. If she had to pick between them, grief would be the emotion she least preferred.

"You got the info on Wiggs?" He didn't probe for more details, but went back to the task at hand.

Thank God. She swallowed, removing the emotional lump from her throat, willing it to oblivion. "Yes."

"Then let's go."

***

Jason flexed his hands against the steering wheel as they passed the old Charming Chemical plant and headed into the woods. There weren't many wooded areas in Iowa, this being probably the largest of them, but it had helped keep Charming quaint and safe over the years.

They drove down a winding road with plenty of foliage on either side, the brush getting thicker and the grass taller as they came to the end of asphalt and the start of gravel. It would take about ten minutes or so to reach the road that led up the side of Mount Charming. No one except for the janitor and one old man had bothered to settle, many years prior, in the woods, the dense forest area being used mostly for camping or hunting. Everyone preferred living in town, but the road held plenty of memories. He and Rose used to take her telescope to stargaze and sled in the winter among other things.

He glanced over at Emma, who nervously picked at her nails, scraping away any trace of dirt from underneath. He understood. Hell, he'd barely calmed down from his discovery of the bodies. People were dying. At least dying to begin with. He hadn't been completely honest with her about the bodies, about how they'd been eaten, left with parts missing. It could be wrong to withhold the information, but he wasn't ready to share his theory of Rose and the sheriff being on people-eating sprees, nor his additional thought that he didn't know if Doc and Gladys would get up and start eating on people, too. One of them had been missing an arm. A startling image flashed in his mind, and he almost gagged, swerving a bit on the road at the same time.

"Are you okay?" she asked, placing a hand on him.

"Images of things I'd rather forget, that's all. Talk to me about other things." He summoned up a weak grin, hoping to set her at ease. She broke the connection between them, concern still etched on her face.

"Well, Dad is going to get Mrs. Hopkins and bring her to our house if possible. There are some reports of more strange things happening and..." She paused, turning her head to look out the passenger side window.

"What? What do you see?"

She shook her head and gave a small laugh. "Is it strange to you that trees are losing their leaves in the middle of spring? And I haven't seen a squirrel, heard birds singing.... No wildlife at all."

He glanced side to side and realized she was right. The majority of the leaves on the trees were the colors of autumn, the bulk of them wilting. Nothing grew here, and Jason rolled down the window to listen for the birds, which always made a racket. The response was silence, pure and disturbing. "I hadn't paid attention to it before, but you're right. This is super strange."

She sighed. "It's got to be tied to this mess. Here's hoping Mrs. Wiggs has some answers. Funny, my dad asked if you were on drugs. Seemed funny to me at the time since we have a huge disaster, and he thinks because we're going to see our old high school janitor, you're smoking reefer."

No, he'd done far worse over the years. His chest went tight, making it difficult to breath. Besides hiding the gnawed bodies from her, he had kept a few other secrets. Would she look at him differently? To those in his group and friends outside of Charming, admitting his addiction came easy. He tugged at the collar of his shirt. Fear of pity and rejection kept him silent around town. It'd be ten times worse if Emma had the same reaction. Either way, the longer he waited to tell the truth, the worse the result.

"It would be funny if it wasn't true." He glanced over to see her jaw slacken and her eyes widen. "You mean you are smoking reefer?"

"No." He readjusted his grip on the steering

wheel again. "No, I'm not smoking reefer." The main thing— complete honesty. The group's coaches always spoke about being truthful all the way. Fuck portraying the situation with falsehoods or denials. "But I was addicted to painkillers. After the accident. I couldn't break the funk, couldn't get over my failure. The pills numbed the knee and, eventually, I used them to numb the misery. Not such a great guy now, am I?"

In her silence, he waited for the disgust, the shock, and the pity that he, the famed quarterback for Charming's only All-State season, had once resorted to using pills to overcome his loss of football instead of having the willpower to pull out of things. The fall had been hard, the recovery even harder. Her letters had made the journey a bit easier, and when his group leader had told him to select a talisman, an object to glorify his goal to stay clean, the words she'd written took the spot.

He flipped the turn signal and slowed down to enter the gravel expanse trailing up the side of the mountain. If memory served him, there was a cabin about half a mile up where Mrs. Wiggs probably dwelled.

"I always thought recovering from something

like a broken bone would be more difficult than everyone made it out to sound." Her tone surprised him. No pity or rejection, only simple understanding. "I'm glad you overcame the addiction, though. What helped pull you out of it?"

Jason let out a sigh. "Letters from this awesome girl who believed my capabilities and smarts ran to more than football, who believed I possessed the ability to become more than a kid on the fast track to a life of small town politics or opening a car dealership. She showed me more compassion than a father and mother bent on social status and appearances. Those words got me off the pills and into therapy."

Another glance at her showed a blush creeping over her cheeks. He wouldn't push the emotions further for the moment, but he did need her to understand the depth of what he felt, why he was so dedicated to the idea of him and her, and why he was not bound to Rose.

"We're here." He made a right and pulled up in front of a small, run-down log cabin.

The tar sheets on the roof were old and in need of a sweeping, and on the front porch that spanned the building sat a traditional rocking chair. An old feeling of creepiness swept over him, similar to the same gut swamping he'd experienced when Rose first wanted to go into the tent at the carnival. Like then, the obligation to escort Emma in, to protect and possibly comfort her, overwhelmed him.

They both got out of the car and approached the cabin slowly. Tense, she rolled her shoulders and shook her upper body as if trying to clear away a physical entity. The entire wooded area was silent. Not a bird, bug, or breeze wafted through the air. He grabbed her hand and squeezed gently in soundless reassurance. She squeezed back and then decided to keep going forward.

They reached the porch and walked up the stairs. Their knock on the door echoed into the forest, and he positioned her behind him in case someone else lived in the cabin instead of Mrs. Wiggs, like some psycho with a gun or, worse, another crazed, cannibalistic citizen. There'd be no chance-taking with another person he cared about.

The door to the cabin creaked open, and he sucked in a breath. From the dimmed lighting, he couldn't tell if anyone was standing there. Then a gnarled hand leaned against the screen door.

"Who's there?" asked a female voice.

"Mrs. Wiggs?" Em replied. She peeked around him, and he let go of his breath as her hand clasped his arm with the same good faith he'd offered her.

"Yes, who is it?"

"It's Emmaline Fay and Jason Prince from Charming. We've come to see you about Rose Briar."

A croaking laugh from the old woman quickly turned into three small coughs. "Well, then you'd better come in and make sure you lock the door behind you. Never know what's wandering around in these woods."

Jason eyed Emma with a look of caution, but she shrugged her shoulders in return. True, they didn't have a choice. This lady remained their best shot at answers. Of course, needing someone still didn't require him to like them. He never had, especially since she'd predicted Rose's demise. If only they'd taken it seriously.

"I'll go first," he said, and, thankfully, she gave in, stepping sideways to let him pass.

The screen door cringed at the pressure of being opened, making more noise than any bit of conversation had thus far. His entrance into the house was anticlimactic, and the sound of Em's steps following closely behind, coupled with the screen door slamming shut, provided additional relief. As he took a minute to allow his eyes to adjust, Emma shut and locked the door. The air smelled of mothballs, cedar, and that distinct scent he'd always attributed to old ladies. Mrs. Wiggs shuffled slowly across the wood floors into the living room at his left, her white hair a beacon in the dim light, so he followed.

She'd just taken a seat as they both finally got into the room. In truth, she still looked the same, except she wore a long black, crocheted sweater and carried a few more wrinkles and liver spots on her hands and face. None the worse for wear and hopefully ready to talk.

"Ma'am, ten years ago you gave Rose a prediction at the Senior Carnival. Do you remember?" Em asked.

"You're the genius. Should I remember?" The old woman asked on wheeze. She reached for a glass of water next to her and took a small sip. "Yes, I remember, and Mr. Football Star remembers, too. Let's get to the meat of it. Something's happened?"

Jason cleared his throat. "Yes, ma'am. Rose is sick like you predicted."

"Not just sick, young man with the manners. She's passing a sickness along, isn't she?"

Now it was Emma's turn to step forward, and she fell to her knees before the old woman.

Jason simply stared into the janitor's gray, clouded eyes. Her head swayed from side to side as if searching for someone. She'd gone blind, and his girl obviously figured as much because she took the old woman's aged hands in her own, providing a sense a direction, of focus.

"Please. Tell us what we can do. You predicted she'd get sick and make others sick, but how do we save her, save everyone?"

A smile appeared on the old woman's face. "You can call me Trudy, dear, and, truth be told, there's no reversal for our poor Beauty. I never saw a cure for the girl, only suffering and something far darker."

"What do you mean?" Em asked, voice laced with pleading.

"The football star knows. He sees the truth of the nasty thing that has consumed your friend." Trudy coughed again, removing one of her hands from Emma's hold.

Jason couldn't meet either of the sets of eyes on him, nor did he want to look for the truth, for the tale. Fear had locked his shoulders in place and made his stomach hard like dried cement, no appetite to speak of. A theory was one thing; to have it be the truth inspired true horror.

"She's a zombie." The words choked in his throat like a death sentence.

Emma gasped. "You mean like a '*BRAINS*' zombie?" The disbelief in her voice, loud and apparent, hit him hard, the first salvo she'd fired at his heart without even being aware. Yet lying never did anyone any good.

"Yes. That kind of zombie."

"I don't believe you. You're making this up. A sick joke." The words sliced through him, emotionally worse than any pain he'd experienced with his broken leg. Drugs had numbed the agony then. Here he received no protection, no way to shield himself from the narrowed, accusatory stare she leveled at him.

Rising to her feet, she crossed the room and backed up to an unused brick fireplace in the far wall. "Let me guess. Rose put you up to some extended scare tactics deal to freak me out so much I won't ever leave here again. Or maybe you...." She pointed a finger at him, the painful, contorted expression on her face breaking his heart, making his chest physically ache. "You didn't do this, but what's happening?"

He stepped in her direction, arms outstretched as if attempting to cage a wild animal. "Its bad luck, pure and simple, and we're stuck in the middle of it." He shook his head. "It's crazy, I know. I wouldn't wish something like this on anyone ever, but if we're right, which I'm about ninety-nine percent sure we are, then Rose is beyond saving."

Defeat entered her eyes, and her shoulders slumped as the truth set in. He remembered the feeling of hopelessness, too. As the tears began to fall, he let her collapse against him for support. She sobbed. He wanted to bring her happiness, but, once again, he had brought pain. "Ah, I see feelings blossom in other corners. The world is not completely dark yet. Still time to save the day," Mrs. Wiggs said.

"How?" Emma's question was muffled, her breath shifting through his shirt. The intimate action gave him hope and faith that they would survive this and have a chance at forming the future he wanted. One with his Em in it. "How do we stop her? Stop this?"

The old woman gave them a yellow-toothed grin. "Just like the movies, dear."

"I've never seen any movies." She made the statement with no shame. Now Jason's jaw dropped.

Emma, his gotta-have-a-chemistry-set, I-cut-up-animals-in-the-name-of-science girl hadn't watched a zombie movie?

"You mean no *Day of the Dead, 28 Days Later, Zombie*?" He stopped as each name gave way to a quick toss of her head. No horror movies. She abhorred horror— he remembered now— and she rarely watched movies anyway. "Then I'll enlighten you. Fire or bullets to the brain are the only surefire ways."

She bit her lip and whispered. "But these are our friends, family."

Those very words gave finality to the task before them. In order to survive, sacrifices would become a common theme. Could they retain a shred of human feeling after shooting the people they'd grown up with as if they didn't matter?

"Sometimes great sacrifices are needed to serve the survival of the world." Mrs. Wiggs' voice cut through the tension, the prolonged sadness, in the room. "Imagine if this spreads beyond Charming. Our world, a horror movie in the making with so many innocent lives lost. Lucky for all of us, the Beauty was so dedicated to the town."

"Such compassion," he said with the full force of

his sarcasm and hatred for the whole ordeal behind it.

"You're right. I don't have much. I warned all three of you about this ten years ago. Now you're in a mess, quibbling over having to clean it up." Trudy's voice dripped with cynicism. "And I can't help. This body is ready to fall to bits. I'd say you got a little bit more luck since I was still alive to answer questions. It's time to fish or cut bait. Either way, whatever you do, I'm bound for death sooner or later."

She sounded angry with them, but he'd be damned if he was going to let her blame him for something out of his control. "You didn't do much to prevent this sickness from happening either. Only gave some half-baked psychic reading, which none of us believed to be true." Once he was done, he immediately regretted the venom that had spewed from his mouth, but looking at the situation from all sides, the old woman looked a bit guiltier.

"It's too late to assess blame." Emma rolled her shoulders back and stood straight. "I'm in this for the fight. If I can't save Rose, I'm willing to find a way to make sure we save everyone we can or at least stop this from spreading beyond the town."

Jason shook off his anger and grabbed Em's

hand, giving it a gentle squeeze. "Then I'm with you. Whatever you need, I'm your guy."

Mrs. Wiggs chuckled. "I always thought the principal's daughter was one of the smartest folks in town. She proved me right. Now I know she's one of the bravest, too. I've got a shotgun behind the front door and a handgun tucked next to me in this chair. Take them with you. Bullets are in the drawer of the stand in the hallway."

Moving beside Mrs. Wiggs's chair, Jason reached for the automatic handgun she'd hidden beside her. He'd shot a gun before, but only during hunting season. Killing animals rode low on the list of hobbies he enjoyed pursuing, and shooting people hit the top of the list aptly called things-I-never-want-to-do. To protect Emma, he'd toss those scruples aside.

"What about you, Trudy?"

"I'll be fine. Honestly, I'm more bones and skin than meat. If they really want a bite, let them have at me." Her voice held a playful tone, but she leaned to the side in her chair, reaching for a pill bottle. "I've got a simpler plan for going out before it gets to that, though. And I'd rather go out on my own terms." Hands shaking, she set the rattling bottle in her lap and looked down at it. No one wanted to die, and knowing the possibilities didn't make the options any easier. He started to move away from her, unable to offer any sound words of wisdom. Even if he'd possessed some, he doubted she'd want them.

Then her hand snaked around his arm with a firm grip. "Football Star, remember.... Once this illness has taken hold, they cease to be those you care about. They are mindless to anything but the feed, the urge. What I've seen has told me this. The spirit within has passed. Only the ravaging shell remains."

A small bit of comfort coursed through him, and he looked at Emma, hoping she'd take the old woman's words the same way. He couldn't tell, though; her focus was on Mrs. Wiggs, and, for a second, he could see the trait that made her and Rose kindred spirits. The inherent ability to care about others and sympathize with them in ways he never could.

"Enough of this standing here. Go, you two, and may luck continue to follow you. Though I'm afraid you'll need more than that."

With those words, Jason went to the hallway, gathered the additional ammunition and the shotgun. When he turned around, the principal's daughter was running her hands along the wooden stair railing leading upstairs, gaze trailing the pictures lining the walls.

"Ready to go?" He opened the front door.

She didn't speak, merely nodded her head and moved in closer.

They got in the car without preamble, Em taking a few more moments to stare at the cabin, no doubt thinking of its occupant, while he settled the guns in the back seat and made sure the safety mechanisms were on.

Driving away put a bit of perspective on things. They were alone, their potential to find help limited to Emma's father and mother and, hopefully, his own. The few hours spent away from town had given way to late afternoon sunshine, which became more visible once they reached the bottom of the mountain and emerged onto the blacktop. Then her tears fell in earnest, her shoulders quaking.

He immediately pulled the car to the side of the road, his gaze darting around the interior to make sure the doors were locked and the mirrors showed nothing behind them. "Come here," he said, reaching for her.

She came without fighting, falling into his arms like it was the most natural thing in the world to do.

He believed the same and wanted to act as her buffer amidst all the craziness. "It'll be all right. You'll see."

Pulling back a bit, she tilted her head, green eyes honing in on his. "How can you say that?"

"Because we have to try and because Mrs. Wiggs never predicted failure." He leaned in and inhaled. Her distinct smell flooded his nose, and he looked back at her face. Her eyes were moist, ready to unleash a new torrent of tears any second, her lips plump and rosy, her cheeks red from crying. She looked so innocent, untainted by horrible times, and each new tragedy kept changing her outlook. He couldn't help wanting to wipe the pain from her eyes just for a moment, so he did the only thing possible. He lowered his lips to hers.

***

The first touch of Jason's lips could be compared to a feather on her skin, but it turned into soft warmth cocooning her. Before she thought to pull away, a hot tongue tentatively touched her flesh and a deafening desire to taste it overtook her. Parting her lips, she allowed that warm heat to sweep into her mouth with a vengeance. All her nerve endings lit up, moisture pooling between her legs. This rivaled the fantasies, all the make-believe thoughts she'd kept hidden away since high school.

His palm slid over her breast, and she moaned into his mouth. He pulled her against him sharply. She wanted more, but the center console, gear stick, and other objects impeded their progress. Their tongue-play made their previous kisses seem like innocent moments. Dozens of dirty thoughts invaded her mind as Jason's fingers found her hard nipple through the bra cup and squeezed. *Ooh.* The pleasure proved so much better when it was his hand and not her own.

Her pocket vibrated. She ignored it while Jason settled both hands onto her shoulders. He pulled her over the console into his lap. If she thought she'd been wet before, her body decided to prove her wrong.

She started her exploration, fast and furious. Desperate to ensure the magic between them didn't fade, she touched his chest through his shirt. Every muscle trembled beneath her fingertips. Pure power shivered under her. When her hands drifted down to his crotch, his erection strained against his pants, his whole body jolting at her slightest caress.

"Em...." Her name slipped from his mouth on a groan. "You're killing me." He captured her lips again.

The vibration went off in her pocket again, and the realization that someone was calling her inspired a sense of dread, killing any sensual thoughts she'd possessed. She pulled back. "Stop."

Immediately, he froze, and she slid back into the passenger seat, pulling the phone from her pocket. The word 'Home' lit up the screen, and she flipped open the cell, afraid to say hello.

"Emma?" Her father's voice, quiet and tentative, scared her silly.

"What's wrong?"

"Everything, honey." He openly let out a sob. "Your mother. She... she's been bitten by Mrs. Hopkins, and I'm afraid she's not going to be herself for much longer."

Emma's heart dropped in her chest. She panicked, breath eluding her. Three days ago, she'd been dreading a reunion with her parents, not planning on losing them. Images of Rose flashed in her mind; the blood shot eyes, the ravaging, euphoric expression as she ripped into the deputy's arm. Her mother would become.... She shook her head. "No, no, no." The word fell on automatic repeat as the memories began to cascade, one after another. From her mother helping select her first-day-of-school-outfits each year to the time when her gran passed and they had spent all day in a blanket fort coloring and cuddling. The sweet, sometimes-overbearing woman who wanted her to be happy and to be home. She'd lose her.

Jason leaned over, and she heard his voice asking questions, but the words never made it through the blood pounding in her ears. He blurred as the tears pooled. Fear, adrenaline— something gave her the strength to hand over the phone to him. Two seconds later, the phone fell in her lap, and Jason threw the car into drive. The only things she recognized were the sound of squealing tires and the smell of burnt rubber.

Chapter Seven

Then the young prince said, "All this shall not frighten me; I will go and see Briar Rose."

Emma walked into the house, fear her close companion. She expected to see her mother rotted away, turning into a monster before her eyes. Instead, Edy Fay sat in a recliner, sweat on her brow and an afghan blanket wrapped around her.

Her grief-stricken father greeted her. Seeing this strong man slumped in defeat, undone before her, twisted her up in ways she didn't want to examine. He'd always been the one in charge, the strong one, leading not only his family, but the school, grades K through twelve.

"Daddy," she cried out as he wrapped her in a bear hug.

"I'm glad you're here, honey. Glad you're safe." His breath pushed against her hair. Safety came from his arms, too. Just like in her childhood. A pained moan came from behind him.

She broke away from her dad and moved to the chair, resting a hand on her mother's forehead. Her skin burned with heat, and she was sweating so profusely Emma took a tissue from the side table to wipe the back of her hand.

Before she could begin to ask questions, Jason pressed the handgun into her palm. "Keep this with you."

She stared at the gun, attempting to tame her fear of the weapon. Shooting guns sat firmly outside her skill set. "But I can't." Killing the woman who'd brought her into the world fell into the impossible category.

"I know, but we have no idea how long it takes for the change to occur. We can't take any chances. What if I'm not in the room?" he asked, trailing a finger down her cheek. He sensed her trepidation, and his quick reaction to comfort her gave her a little reassurance.

"I wouldn't recommend going anywhere. People are becoming crazier by the hour. They move fast, too. The mayor, your father.... I'm sorry." Her dad swiped his eyes with the back of his hand.

"What about him?" The words stuttered out of Jason's mouth as his hand dropped to his side. Then he cocked his head, eyes narrowed on her dad. "Is he all right?"

"On the steps of city hall, he got overpowered. I

couldn't stop them."

The response had the man she'd relied on over the last few days looking a bit shaky. He ran his free hand through his hair and adjusted his grip on the automatic with the other. Shaking his head, he took slow paces toward the door, each step punctuated with a word. "I have to go. Find them. Check on them. I'll be back soon."

She didn't expect a formal good-bye since Jason seemed so out of it. The fact he hadn't screamed or broken down was impressive enough, but distraction could be expected.

Then he stopped, turned, and spoke again, a man willing to protect those he loved and push personal feelings aside to do the right thing. "It'll be sundown in a few hours. I'm going to gather some more ammo and check on my parents. It's my job to protect them." The unsteady tone was now replaced with sheer determination, and he stood straight as if his words were for her alone and included a silent promise that he'd return.

Emma's face flushed at the memory of their kiss not more than twenty minutes or so before and wanted more. The flex of her father's fingers on her shoulder made the naughty thoughts disappear along with a bloom of embarrassment. *Way to keep it together.*

"Be careful," she said, trying to be as strong in her statement as he'd been and hoping those two words and her somber tone told him she'd be waiting.

The need and longing reflected in his deep blue eyes permeated her body, her will. No additional response given, he abruptly turned away, headed for the door. In that moment, her heart clenched, tight, hard, and hurting, in her chest. The dormant feelings she'd locked away years ago had broken free from their cage. If she didn't see him again, if he didn't survive, she'd lose everything.

***

Jason ran to his car like the hounds of hell were chasing him down. A few faraway screams pierced the fabric of the idyllic afternoon. The sun shone bright, a breeze blew through the leafless trees, and the backdrop of country farm houses would've looked stunning in the fall. The inherent evil roaming through Charming permeated whatever sense of safety the town used to offer, leaving lifeless horror in its place—cars abandoned in the middle of the street, shattered windows, and random trash littering the area.

Locked up tight, he began the ride across town, driving slow enough to take in everything around him. No one else was on the road, but just in case, twenty-five an hour seemed the safe bet. He caught some movement off to the left side of the street and pressed on the brakes. Rose was standing in her hospital gown, kneeling over what appeared to be Ewan from the bar. His legs twitched, his eyes filled with pain and his mouth open in a silent scream as if calling for help.

Mesmerized and horrified, Jason watched his ex feast on the one person he'd viewed as competition for Em's affection. Sure, he'd expected to have to prove himself worthy of the girl he wanted, but not by losing Ewan via cannibalistic devouring.

He didn't know what to do, how to react. Rose looked worse since yesterday, her gown covered in different shades of blood, some parts of her once light-blue wrap-around wet, others dry. Her ashen skin had sagged away from her bones. Her eyes had sunken into her skull, her hair a paler blonde than the vibrant color of sunshine it used to be. He slowly reached for the shotgun in the passenger seat. There would be no better time to take a shot. It'd kill a piece of him to shoot his first kiss; hell, his first everything. But for everyone's sake, he'd make the necessary choice.

Bang! The car jolted to the side. Something or someone had bashed into his car from the passenger side. A glance back at his quarry, and she'd risen to a full standing position, looking directly at him. Momentarily paralyzed, unable to react, he willed himself to pull the gun up to his shoulder as one of the back windows shattered.

***

Emma sat in the living room, staring at her mother in the chair. The older woman's head flopped back and forth, signaling her discomfort. Her dad disappeared into the kitchen to make drinks. *Like iced tea makes everything better.*

Two hours had passed with no word from Jason. He said he'd be back. Sun nearly set, she feared the worst. No phone calls had come in from anyone, and conversations with Daddy, brought out the confession that he hadn't talked to anyone since Mrs. Hopkins had inflicted her bite. Her mother and she were his biggest concern, leaving a lot up in the air as to whether the mayor and his wife were one of the diseased or calling in additional help from other towns.

Another moan, more pained this time, came from the chair beside her, and Em watched her closely. She assumed the change would imitate death like it did with Rose before the final turn happened. But since her friend had been patient zero, she couldn't be sure the illness hadn't mutated as it spread. The biggest thing she'd embraced was the chance to say goodbye. Over the last hour, she'd told the woman who'd given birth to her that she loved her, kissed her forehead, and prayed silently for janitor Trudy to be dead wrong about everything.

Her father entered the room with two perspiring glasses of tea. "Here's something cold, sweetie. How's she doing?"

"Worse. Her breathing is getting a bit more labored and slower. I think the time is coming." She took a glass from his outstretched hand.

"I can't believe this. All from Rose. And you're saying Mrs. Wiggs predicted this ten years ago?"

"Yes. I know it sounds crazy, but it's true." She'd shared everything with her father. He was a historian and one of the smartest people she knew. Her silent prayers included him coming up with a solution. Instead, he'd resigned himself to bafflement and anxiousness about the moment when his wife turned into something neither one of them could kill.

"Dad?"

"Yes?" He sat down next to her on the couch.

"Why didn't you call the mayor...or anyone else...after Mom got bitten?" Her dad's behavior held some inconsistencies she'd yet to unravel, and he seemed to have abandoned his usual logical decision-making process completely.

He took a deep breath and slowly exhaled. "I didn't believe anyone else remained unaffected. There were a lot of people at City Hall, including Rose, a couple of other deputies, and a few wandering zombies. By the time the zombie attack was over, we were all in trouble. I couldn't help Jonathon without potentially getting bitten myself. Call me selfish, but you and your mother are all I have. My responsibility."

Tears welled in her eyes. To hear his selfish desires spoken aloud, to believe he had let the friends he'd known for years fall without his aid.... But those words reminded her of how much he loved them, her and her mom, without expectations.

"Oh, Daddy." She set her glass down and launched her arms around him in a hug.

A growl sounded to her left, followed by a crash as the lamp next to her mother's chair fell to the floor. Edy Fay stood, teeth bared, eyes red and feral, and hands spread into claws. A loud screech emerged from the creature's lips, and she launched toward Emma.

Before she could react, her father pushed her off the couch and to the floor. He jumped up and engaged the snarling form of his wife, shoving her backward. "Em, get out of here. Now!" he bellowed.

The warning didn't register, and she got up, searching wildly for the gun she'd placed beside her minutes before. Running her hands along the sides of the couch through the blankets, she found nothing, all the while sounds of snapping teeth and her father's painful exclamations filling the room. She dreaded standing up or turning around without the gun in her hands. Finally, she spotted a small gleam of metal under the couch, next to where she'd landed. Grabbing the gun, she popped up into a standing position. Safety off, she turned to face the struggling forms of her parents, locked together, one attempting to kill and the other merely trying to stay alive.

Bang. Bang. Bang.

Emma squished her eyes shut as the shots rang out in the room. Her finger never touched the trigger of the gun. She opened her eyes to her father with his head in his hands, her mother lifeless on the ground, and Jason, a smoking shotgun still in position against his shoulder. Relief flooded her body at the sight of her personal knight at her side. Her arms fell limp as she moved toward him, the gun clattering against the carpeted floor. She didn't care about anything for the moment except touching him in an effort to remind herself of life.

He lowered the gun and drew her in close. "I'm sorry, Em. So damn sorry."

The words of forgiveness failed to come out of her mouth, but in her heart, he already had it. He was the one person who held the courage to do the very thing she wasn't capable of. She breathed in the scent of him, a scent akin to wellbeing. Then the sound of a gun cocking extinguished any amount of shelter left in the room.

***

On high alert, Jason raised his head, a sense of panic in his gut, the red alert status fairly familiar now, especially after the last two hours, but he never expected the sight in front of him.

"Herb, put the gun down. Everything is fine." Jason tried to keep his voice calm when calm didn't even have a place at his emotional table. Emma's dad was pointing the handgun she'd ditched around the room at them like they'd all joined in on a bizarre game of eenie meenie miney mo.

"No. Everything. Is. Not. Fine," Herb cried out.

The man's hands shook something fierce, and his braver-than-hell daughter stood frozen in shock, jaw gaping. Releasing Emma to attempt to wrestle the gun might result in getting all of them hurt, so Jason decided to continue the verbal approach.

"I know losing Edy is difficult, but that creature.... She wasn't the woman you loved." He squeezed Em tight against him, relishing her warmth and praying for a good way for this to end. "But this girl next to me? This one's still here, and I know you love her, too. So would you mind lowering the gun?"

Herb chuckled, the tone reminding Jason of someone pushed beyond their mental capacity. "You're right, but do I love her enough to end this personal hell? She bit me. My own wife bit me, and now I'll become like her in a matter of hours. I can't live like that."

Shit, the man's declaration sounded like he wanted to kill them all in some savior-suicide attempt. No way in hell he'd let Em go this way. So he moved her behind him, stepping in front to take any bullets launched in their path.

"Emma, I love you. Take care of my girl, Prince." Her father's words were followed by the scrape of teeth against metal and a loud clang as the gun went off in his mouth.

Jason turned abruptly, gathering his girl against him in an attempt to shield her eyes from the worst of it. Then, without looking back at the carnage, he started maneuvering her toward the front door.

Emma dragged her feet and went dead weight on him once they reached the living room entrance. He refused to give up. Her parents were lost to the madness of the situation, but losing her failed to register as an option. As she began to sob, her fists beating against his chest, he picked her up, swinging her over his shoulder in a fireman's carry, and walked out of the house.

"I won't let you leave me, too, Em. I won't let

you."

Chapter Eight

But the moment he kissed her, she opened her eyes and awoke and smiled upon him.

"You know, statistics show the majority of people die from cardiovascular issues or malignant tumors, so I could've expected a heart attack or heart disease to be the silent killer," Emma said as she sat down on the couch in Rose's living room.

Jason seemed to ignore her statement altogether except for his raised eyebrow as he hammered in the last two nails to secure a big piece of wood over the window. The rest of the house already locked up tight, windows covered, doors sealed, the living room window was the last piece of the puzzle.

Now they needed...to do something; exactly what still required discussion and planning. The realization that they were probably the only humans remaining within a hundred miles didn't boost the hope meter at all.

Since Emma had left her parents' house, a numbness had sunk into every fiber of her being, the past few hours of her life replaying over and over in her mind.... Her father's last words, the sound of the gun trigger, the hammer striking, hearing more than seeing her father blow his own brains out—

"Statistics are fine for normal situations, but I can definitely say I hope neither one of those things takes me out," he replied, the last tap of his hammer echoing off the walls.

Such a bold statement when those options sound a hell of a lot nicer. "Oh, so you'd prefer to be eaten by zombies and transformed?"

His eyes fired up at the question. "No. I'd rather die in my sleep of old age, holding the woman I love one last time. Now I'm getting you a drink."

"I don't want one."

"Too bad," he said, walking toward the kitchen, "because you're having one."

"You can't make—"She cut off, realizing the banter lightened the apocalyptic doom, the pain. Everyone in town was a flesh eating zombie or dead, and she'd been ready to have a tantrum.

"Here." He shoved a glass tumbler in her hand.

She raised her eyebrows at the brown liquid sloshing back and forth. "What's this?"

"Indian fire water, woman. Just shoot it. Don't sip."

She went to tilt her glass back, watching as he

shot his, and gave a quick shake of his head afterward. No one ever considered her the experimental one, not even herself, but she didn't want to back down now. A quick chug, and her throat lit up on fire.

"Holy—"A string of coughs emerged next, and he patted her on the back.

"Never did that before, huh?"

She coughed a few more times. "What?"

"Shot whiskey."

"I don't ever want to again. That tasted nasty!"

He laughed. "Well, it's not lemonade."

"I know that, but when you see the guys in the movies, they act like it's nothing to fire away a shot or ten."

"Hollywood lies," he said, laughing again. She couldn't help but join in the laughter, realizing how much their lives were like an insane movie at the moment. He plopped onto the couch next to her, and their eyes met.

"Have you eaten?"

"Except two sips of iced tea and the whiskey shot, I'm on empty."

He reached behind the couch. "Good thing I brought provisions."

A bag of chips and a bottle of water landed in her lap. "Sour cream and cheddar rippled. How'd you know?"

"I remembered." He shook his head in amusement as she ripped into the bag. "You and Rose would send me on the munchies run whenever we had board game night."

She could only nod in agreement with a mouth full of chips, but each hour seemed to reveal another side of him she'd taken for granted in the past. He knew her, took care of her, and appreciated the little things. A decent gulp of water washed away the chips and lingering whiskey taste.

"You're the best as always." Leaning forward, she gave him a kiss on the cheek.

But it wasn't enough, not for her. This could be it, the only chance to be with him, what with the end of the world and all. Sitting silent, even for a few seconds, brought on the visual of her mother dead, and her father giving up; Jason didn't give up, though. He wouldn't. She scooted closer and kissed his lips. Those lips were soft, pliable, and the feelings she'd experienced earlier came back full force. She took the initiative this time, tracing the seam of his lips with her tongue while silently willing him to open to her. He did, and the taste of whiskey and spice hit her hard. He groaned when she sucked on his tongue. The power behind the sound was a heady experience.

Wrapping her arms around his neck, she tugged. He followed willingly as she leaned back on the couch. His hands weren't moving, limp at her sides, as if he refused to give in completely to the moment. No way did he get to back out now.

"What's wrong?" The questions came out on a pant as she pulled away. Damn, she'd never wanted something this bad before.

"We don't have to do this. We can wait." His words said one thing, but the bulging erection against her leg told another story. He wanted her and still tried to play the gentleman.

She ran her palms up his arms and across his chest, exerting barely any pressure and getting a good feel of every muscle. "I think I've waited long enough."

"You've lost your closest friend; now your parents. I want this...us to be more than a way to forget."

"This isn't about forgetting. This is about living dreams." To emphasize her point, she found his pebbled nipple and tweaked it.

Actions always did speak louder than words, and the look of shock on his face made her grin. "I've wanted this a long time. I need—"

Her words were cut off as his lips came crashing into hers, the intensity of his kiss bigger than the previous ones and the joining escalated quickly. Shirts peeled away, pants were shucked, and a two second maneuver with his fingers sent her bra flying across the room. Hands roved, and hot kisses pressed against her neck, shoulders, and lower. He blew a hot breath against her chilled flesh, the spring evening not providing any warmth to her naked body. As he finally made his way to feast on her breasts, he stopped.

She opened her eyes, afraid of what she'd find, but instead of regret, Jason looked her up and down with the ferocity of animal-man desperate to be satiated. "I'm so close to rushing this."

How she wanted to rush, to have him pound inside her as they chased oblivion. Instead, she willed her mind to be quiet and allow whatever he planned to happen as he wished. Then he touched her, fingertips mapping the same route his mouth had taken moments before. He pinched each nipple between his index finger and thumb, causing her to moan and arch upward.

"I love how sensitive you are. It fits."

He traced a path further down her body, skimming along the top of her panties. She couldn't breathe or form words. To say it'd been a while would've been an understatement. The foreplay made her crazy, and when he finally dipped beneath the silk and touched her clit, she jerked. A devious smirk, and he asked, "Okay?"

She only got the chance to nod before his mouth latched onto her nipple, one finger sliding into her channel. A loud moan escaped her lips. Tension, like a chemical solution slowly filling a coiled test tube, began to build. He'd just gotten started, and she'd already reached critical mass; it seemed impossible.

She roamed his back with her hands as he suckled from her, switching between breasts. He slid up inside her with two fingers while his thumb worked her clit, and she began to rock with him, bucking gently beneath his weight. Her orgasm exploded when he bit her nipple with the tip of his teeth. She cried out, and he kissed her, swallowing her cries.

Her focus returned, and she gazed at the grinning face above hers. She couldn't help but return his smile.

"I never knew. I mean I knew, but not with you." Mental forehead slap; that's what she needed. Babbling like a fool who'd been writing with too many dry erase markers.

He leaned in and kissed the tip of her nose. "You haven't known anything yet."

***

Jason slid Emma's panties off, watching the blush spread across her face and down her neck. He was taking it slow and ogling every square inch of her naked body, a Herculean feat considering he'd been aroused too many times to count in the last two days, this being the fourth time today alone. He wanted to enter nirvana desperately, but nothing said inconsiderate like a man willing to slake his own desire without delivering plenty of pleasure to his partner first. For the sake of making this the 'more' he'd originally promised, he'd make sure she received every pleasure possible before taking his own.

With every piece of her clothing completely gone, his focus was drawn to the small black thatch of hair between her legs. He gently ran his hands along her thighs, reaching up to flick her clit. The movements she made, head turning from side to side with each touch, were the ultimate turn-on. If she reacted this way now, he couldn't wait to be inside her, to feel her inner muscles clench against him.

Parting her legs, he positioned himself between them. "Hold onto the couch."

She followed his request, grabbing hold of the armrest behind her head. He wrapped her legs round his shoulders, lifting upward, his breath coming in contact with her sweet lower lips. Then he let his tongue sink within the folds, teasing, tracing, and lapping away. Each movement was designed to stimulate her as much as he possibly could.

She tasted sweet with an edge of salt, the perfect mix and one he'd never forget. Refusing to stay quiet, Em's verbal appreciation of his attentions became louder with each twist of his tongue looping across her small nub and then plunging within. A small prelude to what he'd do to her later. Soon her legs tensed, her back arched further, coming off the couch, and then the dam broke. Her essence flooded his mouth, and he devoured; in fact, refused to pull away until she shuddered and pushed against his shoulders with both hands.

He set her legs down and positioned himself at her entrance. "Are you sure?" If she changed her mind, he'd stop, even though he wanted to plunge forward with every part of his being.

Eyes glazed over, a woman in the last thralls of pleasure, she rivaled any beauty incarnate. "Yes. Please."

The words sounded like a plea of sorts, and how she could still want more after two orgasms stunned him. He ripped the foil on the condom packet and slid it on. Slipping inside her, inch by creeping inch, came close to what pure bliss had to feel like. Tight heat and friction were testing every particle of patience he had.

He groaned. "You're so wet."

A final thrust let him seat himself fully. She gasped and then flexed her muscles as he pulled out, again in a deliberate, leisurely way. He enjoyed the drawn-out tease, allowing the movements to act as additional foreplay before the main show.

Groaning, she locked eyes with him. "I need it harder."

Words any man would die to hear, and from her lips, they were a silky siren's call. He moved back and then pounded forward, grabbing hold of her hips to pull her against him. His crisis grew. Her silken heat a torture device, she would slow his withdrawal then gasp on a sharp intake of breath as he ground back into her. She drove him insane, more insane than any other woman he'd taken to bed. Then she let loose, her head falling back, and he took full control.

As he readjusted his hold to grasp her upper thighs, she shivered beneath him. He intended to get more of a reaction than that. Each new drive forward equated to him physically pulling her to meet him halfway. Flesh slapped against flesh. Soon his breath labored, balls grew tight, and cock went rigid, rock solid hard and ready to release. Relief, pleasure, and satisfaction all wanted equal reign in Jason's mind as he saw stars, his release emerging as he cried out her name.

Running a hand through his hair, he pulled out slowly, careful to move her legs and set them gently against the couch. He detoured to the small bathroom in the hallway and disposed of the condom. Then he soaked a hand towel in warm water, grabbed another dry cloth from the rack, and returned to her. Her eyes were closed, body languid.

"Jason? Oh." She giggled, eyebrows raised in skepticism as he sat by her. "What are you doing?"

"Taking care of you," he replied, pressing the wet cloth between her legs to clean her. Replacing the cloth with the other one, he patted to dry her. The movement caused his cock to stir again, desire he'd leave unsatisfied for now. Taking her twice in one night seemed like pushing things.

"How do you feel?"

"Why would you even ask?" She reached up and touched his arm. He was already sliding into his pants, a bit undone by the intimacy of the moment, living the dream, being with this girl who'd made him believe he could be a hero. He could easily ask the question because their whole world was falling apart around them. If this equated to the I-don't-want-to-die-until-I-experience-this moment, he'd break in two. Regardless, when he turned and met her eyes filled with happiness and her body turning a light blush as he glanced over her nakedness, he pushed aside his insecurities and trusted in the emotional response her body elicited.

"Well, we made love; a little roughly, I might add, and I wanted to make sure I didn't hurt you."

"You couldn't have hurt me. I know you wouldn't."

She pulled her shirt on and grabbed a quilted

blanket from the back of the couch. Jason slipped in behind her, wrapping the blanket around them. He pulled her back against him, and she sighed as he held her. The sound made him long for a chance to repeat nights like this in the future. Insecurities be damned. He wanted the opportunity to be with her indefinitely. Without impending doom.

"Goodnight, Emma."

A kiss against his cheek was the only response received. Content with her nonverbal answer, he closed his eyes and mentally prayed they'd survive.

**

Emmaline stared at the pictures spread across the mantel as she blew on the steaming cup of coffee in her hands. A rooster crowed in the distance, signaling a new day, a day of decisions. After a couple of hours sitting in the recliner staring between Jason's sleeping form and the various objects around Rose's living room, she had figured things out. The passionate night spent in Jason's arms had melted away the tension, the pain, and made her realize she wanted to live her life with this man willing to do anything to save her. The pictures told the same story—dozens of photos with all three of them, swimming, boating, and going to concerts. At each event, he'd not only played devoted boyfriend to her best friend, he'd also protected her. Any tears she'd shed over boys or the lack thereof, he'd proved as much of a support beam as the woman responsible for the carnage ravaging the town.

That thought brought her to the list of ideas on how to rid Charming of the zombie problem. Such a list ran extremely short, and she wasn't sure how they could pull anything off. One thing she still couldn't reconcile— killing Rose, even though she kept trying to convince herself that it didn't matter. The friend she loved was lost forever, but why did the idea of striking her down still hurt so badly?

"Hey, you're up."

Emma smiled at him as he stretched on the couch and sat up.

"Yes, and I made coffee."

He frowned. "Did you have trouble sleeping? You could've woken me."

"No, no trouble sleeping because of anything. My brain was just restless. I guess I just wanted to figure a way out of this."

"Any luck?"

"If you call figuring out a way to attract and kill everyone in town luck then I guess I had some."

He walked over to her and caressed her cheek. She leaned in and laughed as he slipped the coffee cup from her fingers and took a big drink. "Don't beat yourself up about this. It's not like we chose this. Things just happened."

"You're right, but no matter what I do, I'm still torn. Especially about Rose."

"I can understand being torn. But I saw her, and I'm not sufficiently convinced."

She stood up from the chair. "What do you mean you saw her?"

"I saw her, ripping away at Ewan, two blocks from Main Street."

"Did you do anything?" Sweet, unassuming Ewan, who'd twirled her around the floor, giving her a shot at pretending to be more than the second string side-kick who got the pity-me-dates in high school. The tears made another appearance, flowing in a steady stream. She wiped at her cheeks with the back of her hand and waited for Jason to say something.

He growled and set the empty coffee cup on the table. "I'd have done something, Em, I swear, but one of Fowler's zombie deputies rammed the side of the mustang and busted out a back window. I took off. No time to fire off a shot. But Rose stared me down, the look she gave.... Woman's got soulless, devil eyes now."

"I understand. Wish you could've spared him the pain." She walked over to the mantel, running a finger over the prom picture there, across her friend's flawless tresses, immortalized forever. Pulling the trigger seemed an unattainable deed. "I would've hesitated, too. In fact, I did hesitate at my parents'. If it wasn't for you, I'd be a zombie right now."

The truth lie in the fact that neither one of them was perfect. She couldn't hold him to standards she'd be unable to live up to.

"But you're not. So give me a plan?"

"The plan. We lure everyone into the high school and blow it up."

He merely raised an eyebrow and stayed silent. Not wanting to abandon the idea or leave him wondering, she verbalized her thoughts. "We can use what we know about the boiler system in the school along with some well-placed explosive items to weaken the structure and have the building collapse. With a few accelerants, we'd also have a fire on our hands."

"Why not just use the chemical plant?" A valid question, but an option she wanted to avoid.

"We blow that up and hundreds of cubic feet of gaseous chemicals and residue spread through the air. I know we're trying to save the world, but that's like saying if I launch a nuclear weapon here, the long-term effects won't be a big deal. I really want to keep the rest of the population beyond Charming oblivious. A fire at the high school, the possibility of it slowly spreading to the town, and all anyone finds is a reunion celebration gone wrong. Chemical plant, and we expose more people to danger and attention."

The plan sounded really simplistic. Of course, more facets existed, but the quick explanation worked for now.

He stepped closer, reaching for her. "You're forgetting one thing. What about the two people who were here, but suddenly aren't?"

"I've got an answer for that." She leaned in and pressed a kiss to his cheek. "We met up for the first time in ten years on Thursday night." Another kiss, this time on the lips, savoring the taste of coffee and Jason. "Confessed to each other and our parents we were madly in love."

A swipe of tongue across the seam of his mouth, and his arms cinched her waist, dragging her chest in line with his. "Then we drove off into the sunset, headed for Vegas, an all-night chapel, and our happily ever after."

He smiled and devoured her sweet mouth again. By the time he let her come up for air, they were breathing hard and halfway undressed. "You know, I like your thinking. When do we enact this genius plan?"

"Right after you show me how long you've loved me."

Chapter Nine

He told, too, how...many, many princes had come and had tried to break through the thicket, but had stuck fast and died.

"Where are we going?

Jason didn't bother giving Emma an answer as he barreled into a couple of guys with the front of the car. His conscience had acquired additional guilt for sideswiping his father's secretary and the head of Charming First Deposit, but those last two were bullies from high school turned trash collectors.

"We're going on a supply run. You said you wanted to blow up the school, right?"

"That's the plan."

He grinned. "Then we're going to need some heavy duty equipment."

The car came to a stop in front of Charming Hardware. There were a few zombies milling down the street, feeding on a dog. The sight nearly killed him, and he'd wanted to shoot the poor thing. Unfortunately, they needed the distraction if they were going to get the supplies without attracting a crowd.

"Okay." He focused his attention on Emma. "Are you ready to do whatever is needed?"

She looked damn cute with her face screwed up in annoyance. "What's that supposed to mean?"

"That means I'm going to have my hands full. If any zombies wheel around the corner, are you ready to put them down? Remember, their souls are gone."

"I can do this. If it means keeping you alive, yes. I. Can. Do. This." Each word punctuated with a pound of her fist against the dash. *Adorable.* He grinned at her attempts to psyche herself up for what came next. She seemed hell bent on proving her worth, grabbing the nine millimeter from her lap, releasing the safety, and positioning it in her hands like he'd taught her before they left the house.

"Then let's get this show on the road."

No surprise that the door to the hardware store was unlocked, crime never being a big issue in Charming, especially without a bunch of young punk high school students to terrorize the residents. The only downside— they had to lock the door behind them and hope a zombie hadn't decided to roam around inside.

"Let's check each aisle and the back room. Follow behind me," he said, moving into position at the far left row. They progressed down the aisles at a quick pace, stopping every few feet to listen for noises or growls.

"How'd you learn to do this kind of stuff?" she whispered behind him.

"Stuff?"

"The guns, the search procedure. You're not a cop."

As he reached the end of the aisle, he inhaled sharply and then made the turn. *Zombie free*. Then he exhaled. "Well, being in the business of demolition, you take down all sorts of properties. Small, large, condemned, remodel—doesn't matter. You get familiar with police procedure for searching buildings to clear out homeless folk and check structure. Then those cops like hanging out with you and take you to gun ranges on weekends."

"Wow."

Coming to a dead stop, he looked back at her over his shoulder. "Wow, what? See something?"

"Yes, this awesome person who deals with more than explosives. You should've told me sooner or at least given me more details. You don't lead some boring existence in lower Wisconsin."

His pride perked up at her reaction to his

hobbies and life. His parents and Rose had disliked his profession and penchant for hanging out with cops who liked to go shooting nearly every weekend. Yet Emma surprised him again. She always did; another reason why he loved her. *Love*. A word he'd been keeping to himself.

He frowned. "If this mess hadn't occurred, I planned to—hell, I planned a lot of things for this weekend. Then the craziness started."

"I know you had plans, and I did, too. But we're together, and I'm learning you're as amazing as I always thought you were."

Those sweet words made the outcome of this insanity more important than ever. Death still hurt; losing the other people close to him hurt, but he embraced Emma's love in an effort to cleanse. Their future together seemed like fate. He felt it, and he'd make sure he got a chance to enjoy it.

"You're equally awesome. Now we've got all the aisles clear. Let's check the back."

Moving behind the counter, Jason swept aside the solid sheet hanging from a shower rod. Mr. Hicks, the hardware store owner, wasn't a big fan of fancy, his makeshift door another fine example of country chic at work.

The smile Jason wore dropped to a frown as he came face to face with the same Mr. Hicks, red-eyed, with flesh hanging from his teeth, his victim hanging from the big man's arms, completely faceless. The six-foot-four, trucker hat wearing, hardware expert let out a low growl.

Memories of purchasing tree house supplies and receiving advice from good ol' Hickory, as his father called him, flashed through Jason's mind as he raised the gun and took aim. The man he'd once considered a well-intentioned uncle lumbered forward, snarling and gnashing his rotting teeth. Before Jason could fire a shot, gunfire echoed in his ears, and Hickory crashed to the floor.

"I used to be envious of you because the old man wouldn't let me carry tools or supplies out of his shop. Always said carrying stuff fell under a gentleman's responsibilities, not a lady's," Emma said from beside him.

She lowered the gun, and that's when he noticed the tear rolling down her cheek. It didn't matter what lies they told each other—every shot fired, everybody that fell at their hands, would hurt. He lowered his gun and went to hold her, to give of himself. They needed each other to stay sane in the face of so much heartache.

***

Emma possessed a good deal of confidence walking out of the store, gun at the ready and prepared for a zombie ambush. Surprisingly, they made it to the car without incident. Looking out for her lover was Emma's single top priority, even though her heart ached at having put a bullet in another person she'd known since childhood. Just another one on the list of people they were removing from the Earth today.

"You know, I saw someone playing a zombie-killing game back in college. The guy always smiled like a sick pervert and talked about his ninety percent killing accuracy like it was the single biggest accomplishment he'd ever had—"

"Probably was," Jason said with a laugh. She heard the trunk open and the rustle of boxes and plastic canisters as she continued to look every direction. The streets were empty.

"True, but I tried to look at this situation like that one. You can't compare the two. When it's your family, your loved ones, coming at you, their eyes nothing but soul sucking portals to their hunger pangs...it's not like the video games." She shuddered.

The trunk closed with a slam. "All right, we're ready to go."

"Sounds good."

Then she heard the moans, dozens of moans. The visual was worse. At least twenty townspeople were headed toward them. At the very center stood Rose, her hair a lot longer than she remembered and dingy with clumps of dried blood stuck to it. The hospital gown hung from her, dirty and torn. Her exposed skin, devoid of color, displayed various sized pits and oozing boils all over. But what really captivated Emma was the way Rose walked; a slow gait, head lolling from side to side. Intermittently, her friend's head would suddenly stop moving and look straight ahead, the red eyes connecting with hers like a search beam locating a target.

She'd thought fear would've consumed her upon seeing her childhood buddy for the first time since the disaster at the gym memorial, but along with the fear came pity. She also felt an overwhelming desire to run up and wrap her arms around the person who'd shared first crushes, concerts, sleepovers, driving lessons, and dozens of other activities over twenty eight years. Her gun arm fell to her side. The feeling of emptiness without this close friend next to her came to Emma as naturally as breathing, dangerously easy to get wrapped up in.

The crowd came closer with each passing second, and Jason tugged on her arm in attempt to snap her out of her haze. A feral screech rent the air, and Mrs. Hopkins came charging forward. Another tug from beside her, except this time Jason's hand reached for her gun.

"Do something or let me!" His voice, like a beacon in the dark, broke through her concentration on the former prom queen. She snapped her hand away from him, brought the gun up, aimed, and fired. Mrs. Hopkins fell in a heap. This time, when he grabbed hold of her arm, she let him pull her toward the car.

"What the hell happened back there?" His breathing heavy, words labored, he jumped into the driver's side seat beside her. She could tell by the firm set of his shoulders and flushed face, he was pissed.

"I don't know, except the whole thing happened like you described."

"Like I described what? I don't think I described wanting to lose you anytime soon."

She shook her head. "No, I meant like you described Rose. She looked worse, but I just.... I wanted to be with her. Wanted her with me. Does that seem morbid?"

"No, it's natural. I had the same urge when I saw my parents."

"What do you mean?" A knot lodged in her stomach.

"I mean they're gone. I saw them at the house yesterday."

She brought her hands to her mouth. "Why didn't you say anything before?"

"What could I say? You lost your parents, too. Hell, I killed one of them."

"Yes, but you...." Just when she thought all the bombs had been dropped, another emotional nuclear weapon exploded. The nightmare wouldn't be over until everyone in the town was dead.

"If it makes you feel any better, I couldn't kill them." They were in the school parking lot now, car parked, and Jason grabbed her hands. "I wasn't able to go through with it. They were wandering around the backyard, chasing my mom's cat, and I locked the doors behind them. They wandered off within minutes."

"What's the difference between them and mine?" She didn't mean to sound cruel with the question. Nonetheless, he looked away, hurt by her tone.

"A personal connection to our own parents. Why couldn't you shoot Rose?"

She sighed, edging a finger underneath his chin to bring his gaze back to hers. "A personal connection, and, to be honest, we need to end her with this explosion. I could bring myself to shoot just about anyone here except for her. I froze once, and I'll freeze again. There's some sort of binding power between us. That's the only way I can describe it."

"I understand." He leaned in and kissed her forehead. "But that's why love is a great thing. It gives you someone to share the burden of responsibility with, and I plan on lightening your load."

"I love you." An awkward time to give such a proclamation, but she wanted it said in case the worst occurred. No sense in denying the re-awakening of her feelings either. Life continuously proved too damn short.

He smiled. "I love you, too. Now would you care to cover me while I unload all this stuff?"

Chapter Ten

'Til at last she came to an old tower around which there was a narrow staircase ending with a little door.

"Hand me a cap-thingie, will you?" Jason pointed at the pack of electrical grounding caps on the floor. Emma grabbed a cap with one hand, the gun still in the other, and placed it in his. Once the last piece was put in place, the whole building would finally be wired to blow.

"Explain to me how this works again." She went back to looking for zombies, glancing left to right down the hallways.

He loved how they worked together. After three hours of intensive labor, surprisingly, only a few zombies had gotten in the way. The sad part— he'd stopped referring to the people of the town as people he knew. Now they were just zombies.

"All right." He stood up, dusting off his jeans. "I've placed a line of accelerant around the entrances to the gymnasium. Once we turn on the music from the AV booth and get everyone in here, we fire one bullet to ignite it. This will prevent anyone from leaving, and we let them burn or pick off what we can with the guns."

He paused for a second, thinking he'd heard something from behind him, but there was only silence. Stuffing his all-in-one tool into his pocket, he grinned. "Then the easy part. I've rigged everything so we can collapse all outside entrances with the push of two buttons."

"You're a genius." She flung her arms around him and locked on tight. A rush of contentment passed through him, and he would've been happy stuck in this position forever. Being with her meant more than anything, and in two hours, they'd be free. Based on his wristwatch, the sun was already beginning to set. The only thing left to do was hightail it to the AV room above the gym and start making noise.

"Thanks, but you're not so bad yourself. Ready to get the party started?"

She sighed, stepping back. "Are you sure we're going to get everyone?

"I'm sure, but if you think we missed anyone we can stick around for a few hours afterward and check things out."

His words were meant to relieve the tension

building around them, but when she handed him the gun and started pacing, his belief in the whole plan started to unravel. "Don't you feel sick talking about maiming at least a hundred bodies like we're assembling a tree house or putting on some sort of performance? Every time I think I'm okay, you say something else, and then I'm not," she said.

There was a point to her thoughts, and he believed the same, to an extent. At least he didn't think their behavior to be normal, hadn't from the moment Rose bit into the sheriff.

"I feel sick about all this, yes, but, again, we don't have a lot of options here. So how can I make this better for you? How do I make this all right?"

She stopped pacing, and walked up to him. "Just keep reminding me that we're on the same page. Then I don't feel like I'm going insane or that I'm the only one seeing all this as wrong."

"It's more than wrong. Honey, it's a catastrophe, and we've got to put a stop to it. When you're backed into a corner, the only way out is to give up or fight. I almost gave up once with my knee, and I'm not doing it again."

He snagged her hand and gave the back of it a quick kiss. If there were time, he could invent countless ways to spend the evening hours with her, but procrastination only left room for them to screw up or become complacent. With the whole town zombified, it was possible that, after tonight, the hunger pangs would send zombies beyond Charming's borders.

"Em, if I had the ability to change all of this, I would. I'd do anything for you. Don't doubt that please." He scanned her face, looking for a sign of doubt, mistrust, or anything to give him an idea of the true thoughts rambling through her mind. If she wanted to question things, he'd let her; their humanity required it.

"I don't." The words rang true, her eyes shining without doubt or hesitation. They were ready to go.

"Then let's get to it."

***

The music blasted from the speakers in all four gym corners. The spinning disco ball gave the room a high school dance setting. Emma remembered all the dances and how she'd spent most of them up here, playing deejay. Now she stayed up here out of a need for survival; a little ironic. Zombies filed in at a steady pace, and she'd already counted seventy-five residents of the town. Three-fourths wasn't bad after one hour since they didn't seem to move very fast unless food presented itself.

They ran into walls and each other, snapping their teeth a bunch. The stench of decay quickly became a bit overwhelming.

"Have you seen Rose?" Jason's question came on a whisper as he sat down in a chair next to her.

"No. She hasn't made an appearance yet, but I expect her. Other than her, the sheriff, and Doc, everyone else is here, including your parents."

He didn't react, but merely peeked over the edge of the AV booth and looked around. Watching loved ones act like mindless fiends, he found the sight hard to look at for more than a second.

"The whole thing reminds me of drug addicts, people distracted by everything until you put the one thing they want in front of them and then try to take it away. Only this is ten times worse because you can't reason or fight."

"True. A battle you can't win."

He laced his fingers with hers. "I plan to at least win some part of it."

He leaned in to kiss her, but, at that moment, she

caught sight of the captivating woman before whom all the other zombies cowered as if she were royalty.

"She's here."

Emma couldn't look away from her again, the image reminding her of prom night and Rose's regal entrance into the dance. The same scene, just more blood and decay involved.

The cock of a gun broke her focus on her friend. "What are you doing?"

"No time like the present. That's everyone, right? The sheriff and Doc just entered through the other door."

"Yes, but can't we—"

"You know we can't." His eyes turned sympathetic. "Waiting gives one of them the opportunity to get away. I know what seeing her does. Remember, you're not the only one suffering."

He didn't wait for additional comments, just aimed and fired. A small roar exploded as the can of paint thinner caught fire and a blazing ring quickly spread around the room. Screeches and roars of pain sounded at once, filling her ears with an awful buzzing. The smell of decaying, burning flesh became worse as more bodies ignited, causing her nostrils to burn.

Jason and Emma just stood in silence as the plan took hold, zombies burning when attempting to escape and spreading their flames to others, similar to how they'd spread the disease. She gripped Jason's hand, and he squeezed back. They fed each other strength and love to keep from becoming two emotional messes.

The end was near, the majority of the bodies covered in an orange and yellow blaze, when Rose leaped over one of the flames and skidded to a stop outside a gym door. A glimpse of her stained dress and long hair was the last Emma saw of her.

"Damn. Come on. She's getting away." She ran down the stairs, making a quick check, once she reached the bottom, for other potential escapees. Then she charged off into the night after Rose.

***

"Where are you—" Jason cut off as his girl disappeared down the stairs. He grabbed a handgun and rifle and took off after her, but by the time he'd reached the bottom, she'd disappeared.

Torn between going after her and securing and blasting the doors to the school as planned, he settled on cleaning up the mess in front of him. The wrong choice could cost him, but the world's future rested in his hands for the moment.

Bowing his head, he silently prayed his sweet Em would remain safe until he could follow her. Depleted of regrets and hesitation, he charged off to start chaining doors. At least there'd only be only one zombie to contend with once he finished.

Chapter Eleven

Then he went on still further, and all was so still that he could hear every breath he drew....

Emma's breath came in heavy pants, and she finally came to stop at the edge of town. She'd followed Rose, but couldn't find a trace of her. She had also forgotten the most important thing, her gun. Running down main roads and cross streets seemed futile at this point. With over thirty empty buildings, there were plenty of hiding spots, except she'd counted on her friend being hungry.

The outline of Charming Chemical lingered in the background, only a half mile of open field separating it from the town. Inoperative, it really stood out as an eyesore, another decaying symbol of what the town had become. From the crumbling walls to the dead overgrowth that crept across parts of the bricks to the rusting metal—who knew what chemicals the building leaked into run off water? She took a couple of deep breaths to slow her heartbeat, and then a warning growl rent the air.

Rose stood at the opposite end of the street, a good twenty feet away. Now the debate began. Should she run or try to find something to climb? Running seemed like the more logical choice because trees were scarce, and she failed to control the ability to scale buildings with her bare hands. Her only hesitation lay in the inability to predict how fast her friend's zombie body could react.

Another growl, and Rose took two steps forward, her head swinging. She appeared agitated, hands clawing at the air for something, anything, to grab hold of. It was heartbreaking to see her like this, and Emma experienced a deep, desirous urge to help until the dead nurse's screech rent the air, deafening and unnatural. The sound confirmed a lack of humanity and freed the guilt she'd harbored.

Not missing a beat, she turned and ran toward the field. She'd give everything to get to the chemical plant. Grabbing her phone from her pocket, she dialed Jason's number.

"Where the hell are you?" The question possessed a small amount of irritation.

"What, no hello?"

"Not when you run off and leave me behind. Are you all—"

"I'm leading your ex to the chemical plant." She blurted out, cutting him off. "There might be a way to trap her there. Do you have any more blasting supplies?" A snarl sounded beside her, and she wanted to look, but knew it would only slow her. The goal—to keep running, don't look back, and hope she'd be faster than a zombie; the best possible plan.

"I've got the supplies. I can be there in fifteen."

"Great." The word escaped on a breath.

"Don't do anything crazy, okay?"

"I think I passed crazy when I thought I could outrun a zombie over half-a-mile. This isn't a sprint like the ones I medaled in back in track." Although her attempt to make a joke and keep her feet moving was feeble at best, there was truth there. Getting old changed things in big ways. The call ended, and she shoved the phone back into her pocket.

The entrance to the plant only a few feet away, she scanned for closed fences; surprisingly, there were none. Again, the small town mentality had kept everyone from locking things up. As she got closer, the sound of Rose's movements diminished. She noticed graffiti on a few walls. Rusting pipes and cracks in the concrete acted as further signs the buildings could not stand immune to Mother Nature.

Her legs were like dead weight, but, with every step, she summoned more strength to keep going.

She didn't want to be like everyone else in the town, didn't want to desire the taste of human flesh. Dashing into the first building, she wove down the halls, searching for anything to protect herself or for a room to hole up in. All the offices had windows, which wouldn't benefit her. Charging through one set of double doors led her to the main plant floor. Big vats of liquid nitrogen loomed in front of her. She knew they were filled since Rose's big push for grant money had involved using the funds to sell or disperse the remaining chemicals in the plant that posed a danger to the town. Outside the doors, she heard a crash, most likely her friend come to find her. Emma looked around, desperate for a place to hide. Then she saw the ladder against the right wall.

Hand-over-hand, she climbed up the ladder to the catwalks. Once on top, she carefully guided herself through the railed metal walkways carefully positioning herself between two of the nitrogen vats. She saw the evidence up close; these were extremely dangerous with only glass tops to keep the liquid from being exposed.

The double doors burst open, and a roar like that of a feral cat signaled the zombie queen had finally caught up. Emma hunched down on the catwalk, pulling close to the rail in a poor attempt to hide. Another growl right beneath her. Her friend looked at her with those hungry eyes. Emma couldn't move, frozen, and without a weapon.

Rose hunched low and then pushed off her feet into the air, the move purely supernatural. With hands latched onto the cat walk, the she-zombie pulled herself on to it. Emma stood, fear sinking deep into her bones. She couldn't think, only edging herself further away while her friend snarled and scratched at the air, moving slowly toward her. No way would this crazy high-rise be the end, but how could you kill a person you loved with everything in you?

As her childhood companion charged without warning, Emma did the only thing she could do. She took a stance and braced for impact. Grabbing hold of Rose's slimy, lifeless arms before any zombie claws could reach her, she twisted to her right, using her momentum to drag Rose with her. They both went over the side, and, naturally, Emma let go of her attacker, arms waving widely in an attempt to locate stability. She screamed. *This is it*.

***

Two guns at the ready, Jason burst through the doors, resigned to the fact that he would have to kill his ex. Then he heard the scream above him. Running between the huge chemical vats, he caught sight of Em holding onto the catwalk for dear life. Zombie growling and the sound of cracking glass also echoed through the room. He couldn't see where Rose was, though.

"Hold on, Em." He turned around, heading back to the catwalk ladder. What turned out to be only a few seconds of climbing felt like forever, but then he grabbed her hands, pulling her toward him. She leaned into his embrace, and he soaked up the closeness. Their time apart had been pure agony.

Their tender moment got cut short, though, as the sound of fracturing glass grew louder. He looked down at the chemical vat. Scratching at the vat lid, his prom queen stared up at them. She kept attempting to stand, oblivious to the damage she' caused. A final twist of her body broke the lid, and she fell inward with a screech. He wanted to lean over for a closer look, but his girl pushed against him.

"We have to go. Now."

He let her lead the way as they scrambled off the

catwalk and out the doors. Once near the outer hallways, he sealed the doors and started placing the explosives. Her only request was no fire, which would make things worse. After the events of the evening, he'd expected to feel relief now that they'd overcome the final obstacle. Instead, numb became his word of choice as he placed the last of the wiring and inserted the detonator

"We're all ready to go." He walked toward her. She leaned against the car, head turned up to the sky. Her eyes held a lost look, a mirror of what he felt. "Are you ready?"

"Yes, I think I am."

"I'm going to blow the doors. What's the chance the nitrogen will evaporate?"

"Slim chance. We're cutting off the air. Released liquid nitrogen also removes oxygen. I can only hope the chemical cuts off brain function."

The words sunk deep. A chance Rose survived remained. "She could still be alive."

"Possible, but doubtful." She looked at him and frowned. "The only way to know for sure is to dissolve the very thing that stopped her."

"So safe way is to leave and not look back."

"The best option, obviously," she said, looking

away from him again.

How do you wipe the sorrow away? The question plagued him as he collapsed the lever. Several small concussions followed by the sound of crumbling rock signaled the entrances were closed.

"Emma, can we ever—" His words were cut short as she ran to him. Enveloped in her arms, the pain ebbed.

She stared into his eyes with a smile. "Yes, we can. Let's get out of here."

About the Author

Landra Graf consumes at least one book a day, and has always been a sucker for stories where true love conquers all. She believes in the power of the written word, and the joy such words can bring.

In between spending time with her family and having book adventures, she writes romance with the goal of giving everyone, fictional or not, their own happily ever after.

Also by Landra Graf

Raven Pirate Assassin Spy

What You Need

What You Crave

What You Want

What You Desire